WAKE UP LOVE

SURAJ KARKERA

Made with ♥ on the Notion Press Platform
www.notionpress.com

For

Mom and Dad.

My Sis Rati

and

My cute nieces Shloka and Arohi

Contents

ONE

GO GOA GONE.

It was Thursday, and a long weekend loomed ahead, with Friday being a public holiday. Nikhil and his friends had their routine plans, they decided to head to Goa. This was a frequent getaway for them; whenever such opportunities arose, Goa was their go-to destination.

At 31 years old, Nikhil worked for an IT company. Busy packing his hiking bag, he suddenly realized he needed a few essentials for the trip and decided to make a quick stop at the convenience store.

Exiting his apartment, Nikhil stepped into the lift, only to realize he needed to call his boss for some extra leave. His plan with friends involved taking an extra day off on Thursday and another on Monday, ensuring a glorious three-day stint in Goa. Inside the lift, Nikhil swiftly decided to message his boss about the leave. Bluntly, he typed, "I won't be coming today as I am not keeping well; I got the flu." After hitting send, Nikhil strolled out of the building and into the parking lot, heading towards his scooter.

Nikhil owned a classic red and white Lambretta, a sight to behold. As he reached his scooter, he noticed a young girl from college standing beside it.

The girl looked at Nikhil and inquired, "Is this Lambretta yours?" Her question caught Nikhil off guard, and before he could respond, she exclaimed, "I love this vintage red and white scooter. Where did you find this?"

Nikhil replied, "This is my mom's scooter. My dad gifted it to her after they got married. Now, since they both are no more, I have inherited this gift of love."

The girl, with a contagious smile, couldn't take her eyes off the vintage beauty. Nikhil, captivated by her enthusiasm, was about to ask for her name or which floor she lived on when she entered the building, leaving him wondering.

Upon his return from the store, Nikhil, in a moment of panic, couldn't find his keys. After a frantic search, he discovered them in the back pocket of his jeans. The scare made him realize it was a close call; had he lost the key, he would have been stranded outside. Deciding to be smart, he opted to give a spare set to his neighbor. It was the first time he had interacted with them, making this a novel experience in getting to know the person next door.

Nikhil rang his side neighbor's doorbell, and a pretty looking middle-aged woman answered the door. She gazed at him without uttering a word.

Nikhil, attempting to break the silence, greeted her, "Hello, Ma'am. I am your neighbor, and my name is Nikhil."

The lady continued to look at him, maintaining her silence. After a brief pause, Nikhil continued, "I want you to keep my house keys, just in case I lose mine."

Before she could respond, her daughter entered from inside.

"Oh my God, it's you," the girl exclaimed. Nikhil was surprised to see her. He thought to himself, 'The scooter girl, what are the odds? Out of all the floors, not only does she end up on my floor, but she happens to be my neighbor.'

The girl's mother asked her with surprise, "You know him?" The girl replied, "Mom, remember I told you about a guy who has a Lambretta scooter?"

Her mom, with a hint of disapproval, said, "That piece of junk is his?" The girl defended, "Mom... It's a vintage scooter."

She pushed her mom behind and stepped out of the door, extending her hand for a shake, and said, "Hi, I am Priya."

Nikhil gazed at her, noticing she held a selfie stick with a GoPro attached to it. Politely, he shook her hand and introduced himself, "I am Nikhil." Intrigued, he pointed at the GoPro and asked, "What's that?"

Priya replied, "It's a video camera. I am a Vlogger." Nikhil nodded in understanding, saying, "Oh, okay."

Priya suggested, "You should subscribe to my channel. Do you have your phone on you?" Nikhil affirmed, "Yes," taking out his phone and handing it to Priya.

However, Priya's mother interjected, expressing impatience, "Well, I've got things to do. I am going in. Don't waste your time with her." With that, she took the key from him and retreated into the room.

Meanwhile, Priya subscribed to her channel on Nikhil's phone, encouraging him, "Now you can watch my videos on the go."

Nikhil glanced at his phone for a moment before tucking it back into his pocket. Curious, he inquired, "Are you in college?"

Priya confirmed, "Yes, I am in my second year." Nikhil then shared his plans, "Well, it's a long weekend. I am off to Goa on a trip with my friends. While traveling, I'll watch your vlogs."

Priya blurted out spontaneously, "Can I have your scooter for this weekend, please?" Nikhil hesitated before replying, "No, your mom will kill me."

Priya persisted, "Listen, I have a proper license, and I drive my friend's motorcycle. So, a scooter is safer than a bike, and I'll take good care of it."

Nikhil couldn't believe his ears, but in the recesses of his mind, he also liked Priya, so he couldn't refuse. Finally, he relented, saying, "When I come back, I want you to come to me and give my keys back. Don't make me run after you, and not a single scratch, or I'll make you pay for it."

Priya agreed with a confident thumbs-up, saying, "Deal." Nikhil, still somewhat reluctant, handed her the keys.

After handing over the scooter keys to Priya, Nikhil grabbed his bag and set off for the trip. His friends had told him to wait at a coffee shop where they would pick him up.

Samrat, a 28-year-old chef at a local fine-dine restaurant, was almost done packing his suitcase. As he prepared to leave, he heard a commotion of greetings in his living room. Curious, he took a peek and saw that some guests had arrived.

In a hurry, Samrat grabbed his suitcase and tried to make a quick escape, knowing his parents would likely make him wait. His mother called out, "Where are you going in such a hurry?"

Samrat replied, "Mom, I've told you about this trip. I'm running late."

His mother insisted, "Wait, leave your suitcase there and come here. It will only take 10 minutes. Besides, even if you're a couple of hours late, your friends will still wait for you."

Growing agitated, Samrat said, "Mom, just 10 minutes, and I'm already a couple of hours late."

His mom smiled sarcastically, "You're always the first one to arrive. I'm sure you're leaving a couple of hours early."

"Wow, this is embarrassing," Samrat thought to himself as he glanced at the guests. A pretty girl with big innocent eyes stared at him, and Samrat found himself unable to look away. It was as if those eyes were casting a spell on him.

Samrat's mom introduced him to the girl's parents and then to the girl herself. "This is Varsha." Samrat's mom said. Varsha, feeling a bit shy, managed a smile and greeted with a simple "Hi."

Samrat's mom continued, "I hope you've realized by now that they are here to see you for their daughter, Varsha. They wanted to come on Sunday, but since you planned this trip without asking me, I had to call them before you left."

Samrat, a bit surprised, said, "Mom, you could have at least told me about it."

His mom responded, "Beta, marriage, love, and women are full of surprises."

Understanding that this time his mom was determined to arrange the marriage, Samrat quickly devised a plan. "Can I show Varsha my room?" he asked.

Varsha's parents approved, and Samrat led Varsha into his room.

Samrat's room was small, with a single bed, a computer desk, a small chair, and an abundance of international cooking books.

Varsha's eyes fell on a huge Gordon Ramsey Hell's Kitchen poster on the wall. She looked back at Samrat and pointed at the poster, saying, "Really?"

Feeling a bit awkward, Samrat responded, "I have a Nigella's poster too." He then guided her to the other corner to show her the additional poster.

Varsha glanced at Samrat and teased, "I guess you're a nerd, a chef nerd, if that's even a word." She took a seat on his bed, while Samrat settled into his small chair.

An awkward silence hung in the air until Samrat spoke up, saying, "Listen, don't get me wrong, but I don't want to get married like this."

Varsha, with her already big eyes widening even more, asked, "Like this?"

Samrat clarified, "I mean, you're pretty, but I don't prefer arranged marriage." Varsha questioned, "Then what do you prefer?"

Samrat explained, "I prefer to fall in love with an independent girl who has a career of her own. Besides, I feel I am not ready for marriage in general."

Another weird silence followed, and then Varsha said, "I understand what you mean. Well, that sucks because I liked you. Anyways, thanks for being honest."

Samrat apologized, "I am sorry, but could you do me a favor?" Varsha inquired, "And what's that?" Samrat requested, "Could you reject me? Because you look good, and if I reject you, then my mom will think I am crazy. So please, after you go home, tell your mom you didn't like me, and she'll tell my mom."

Varsha gave a small giggle and then smiled.

They stepped out of Samrat's room, and his mom shot him a questioning look. "So... what's the verdict?" she asked.

Samrat replied, "Mom, I'll tell you when I get back. For now, I am getting late." He greeted the guests and hurriedly left with his suitcase.

Meanwhile, Nikhil had been waiting at the coffee shop for half an hour, growing increasingly impatient. Just when he was about to give up, Samrat finally showed up. "You're late," Nikhil remarked. Samrat said, "You won't believe what happened."

On the other side of town, Vedant, a 22-year-old guy, worked alongside his dad in a massive, tricked-out garage. His passion lay in modifying cars, bikes, or any vehicle that crossed his path. It started as a hobby, but soon customers began seeking him out to give their old four-door cars a makeover, transforming them into sleek, red, shiny two-door sports cars. Vedant had become quite skilled at it, having successfully completed numerous jobs for satisfied customers.

Vedant had borrowed his dad's SUV for the trip, already running late and opting for a shortcut. As he maneuvered through the narrow lanes, he encountered an unexpected roadblock, a truck unloading furniture and household items, a clear sign of someone recently moving in. Annoyed by the delay, Vedant brought his SUV to a halt and approached the truck, where the driver was overseeing the unloading.

"How long will it take?" Vedant inquired, a hint of impatience in his tone.

The driver glanced at Vedant and then at his SUV. "I'm not sure; there's still a lot of stuff in the truck," replied the driver.

Frustrated, Vedant realized there was little use in talking to the driver and decided to approach the homeowner to expedite the process.

Entering the bungalow, Vedant's eyes were captivated by a beautiful lady. She stood draped in a transparent pastel blue chiffon saree, complemented by a baby pink sleeveless blouse. The loose end of the saree gracefully swayed in the light breeze, mirroring her long, flowing hair. Vedant couldn't help but be entranced. A thin gold band adorned her waist, seamlessly blending with her caramel complexion. Her smoky eye makeup and a tiny mole just an inch away to the left side of her lips added to her allure.

The lady interrupted the trance Vedant was in. "Yes, how may I help you?"

Vedant, startled, snapped back to reality and approached her. "Well, my car is stuck because of this truck," he explained.

The lady inquired, "Where are you off to?" Vedant replied, "The coffee shop on GT Road. I have to pick up my friends; we are off to Goa."

The lady asked, "Why didn't you go by the main road? You would have reached by now."

Vedant defended his choice, saying, "This was a shortcut."

The lady responded wisely, "Most shortcuts end up taking longer than the longer route. Well, don't worry; the loading is almost done."

The driver and loaders were finishing up, getting ready to leave. The lady locked the front door of her bungalow.

Vedant, curious, asked, "Didn't you just move in?"

The lady explained, "Yes, but it's my brother's 1st death anniversary, and I want to be with my family. They have arranged a ceremony to cherish his loving memories, so I am off to Kerala for this weekend. I'll unpack everything when I get back on Monday."

Vedant, seizing an opportunity, asked, "Are you leaving now?"

The lady replied, "Yes, I have to reach the station before the train arrives, so that I don't have to rush things."

Seeing a chance to be of help, Vedant suggested, "The station is on the way. I don't mind dropping you, and picking up my friends won't take much time."

After a moment's thought, the lady agreed, "Okay." As the truck driver moved on, the lady picked up her small suitcase and dragged it toward Vedant's car. Vedant opened his door, and the lady opened hers. Before getting in, Vedant said, "Hi, I'm Vedant." The lady smiled and responded, "Hi Vedant, I'm Malavika."

Nikhil and Samrat waited for Vedant, and to their surprise, they saw him pulling over next to them with a lady in the car.

Samrat quipped, "You're late." Nikhil added, "He just waited for half an hour, but I've been here for almost an hour now."

Vedant apologized, saying, "Hi, guys. Sorry for being late, and guys, this is Malavika. I'm dropping her off at the station on the way."

The boys exchanged glances, they stuffed their bags into the rear seats of the SUV and took the seats behind Vedant and Malavika.

As they drove, silence filled the car, and Vedant couldn't help but think, 'The moment she gets out of the car, that would be the last of it. How will I meet her again?'

Malavika broke the silence, "So, you boys often take this trip?"

Vedant replied, "Yes, we plan this weekend trip to Goa every four months. We search for a hidden retreat spot in Goa, spend three days there, and return fresh and recharged. We do this three times a year."

Curious, Malavika asked, "So, how did it all start?"

Vedant shared, "The three of us lived in the same building, like family friends. I was the youngest among us. As time passed, our parents moved to different locations, but our families stayed in contact. When I started college, the three of us became close friends, and that's how we started this Goa trip ritual."

As they chatted, Malavika noticed the station approaching. "Looks like the station has arrived," Malavika remarked.

Vedant brought his car to a stop close to a footpath. Vedant, thinking quickly, said, "So, you'll be back on Monday."

Malavika confirmed, "Yes."

Vedant continued, "We'll be back on Monday afternoon. We can help you unpack your stuff at home, and I'm sure the guys will help as well, right guys?" Vedant looked at Nikhil and Samrat. The two exchanged glances but didn't say a word. Malavika responded, "Oh, don't worry. I'll manage. You need rest after all that partying in Goa, and I'm sure you need to go fresh to the office the next day."

Vedant gave the guys a stern look. Samrat finally spoke up, "No worries. We got your back. Glad to help. We'll be there on Monday." A smile spread across Vedant's face.

After thanking Vedant for the ride, Malavika headed towards the station, and the boys continued their journey to Goa.

After wrestling with the chaotic city traffic, the guys finally hit the open highway, and it seemed like smooth sailing from there. Vedant takes the wheel, opens the sunroof, and rolls down the windows, inviting in the warm sunlight and refreshing breeze.

Samrat, chilling in the back seat, says, "Hit the music, Nikhil, you know the protocol."

Nikhil, seated next to Vedant, dives into his phone to find their go-to song. The inaugural track for their car audio is none other than the title song from the movie 'Dil Chahta Hai.' It's a ritual for them, a prelude before any other tunes.

The reason behind this choice lies in the movie's tale of three friends embarking on a road trip to Goa. This specific song plays when they cruise in a convertible, with the sun kissing their faces and the wind tousling their hair.

Recreating that cinematic moment floods them with nostalgia. It's not just about the music; it's about reliving the essence of a film that captured the spirit of their own adventures. As the melody fills the car, they find themselves transported back to the carefree vibes of friendship and open roads.

On the journey, they made a pit stop for lunch at an open-air restaurant, commonly known as a dhaba, serving local delights.

While indulging in their meal, Samrat, glancing at Vedant, remarks, "Do you know what this guy did?" pointing at Nikhil.

Nikhil, with his mouth full, halts his munching and looks at Samrat, wondering what's being chatted about.

Vedant, intrigued, asks, "What did he do?"

Samrat spills the beans, "He gave his Lambretta keys to a teenager."

Nikhil, defending himself, says, "She's nineteen."

Vedant, looking at Nikhil, exclaims, "What the...? Are you trying to impress a college girl?" He then turns to Samrat and queries, "How do you know all this?"

Samrat casually replies, "You were an hour late, so we were gossiping to kill time."

Then, turning to Nikhil, he adds, "And dude, nineteen is still a teenager. In fact, you should see someone like Malavika; she looks like someone of your age, plus she's a beauty."

Hearing this, Vedant interjects, "Whoa, hold on, I have dibs on her."

Samrat chimed in, "My-my, what do we have here? I thought Nikhil was crazy for dating a college kid, but now we have a 22-year-old in love with a 30-year-old woman?"

Nikhil quickly clarified, "I am not dating any teenager; I just lent my scooter to her, and I am not in love with her, so please stop this."

Vedant added, "Listen, I really don't know anything about her; maybe she has a boyfriend."

To which Samrat teased, "Or she's married and has two kids." Vedant shot Samrat an annoyed look, visibly fuming.

Nikhil, attempting to shift the attention, said, "By the way, do you know what foolish thing Samrat did before leaving home?"

Anticipating the revelation, Vedant asked, "What?"

Samrat, with a grin, responded, "Guys, I know; you both are trying to corner me now."

Back in the car, they zoomed down the highway, with Nikhil at the wheel this time, Vedant next to him, and Samrat in the back.

Vedant turned back from his seat and said. "I don't believe this; you said no, you rejected her?"

Samrat explained, "It was an arranged marriage thing. I want to fall in love, have a girlfriend, and then get married. I want an independent, smart girl, so I said no."

Nikhil, curious, asked, "Oh, so you knew her?"

Samrat clarified, "No, I didn't even give her a chance. I just told her to reject me."

Vedant, puzzled, inquired, "Why did you tell her to reject you?"

Samrat confessed, "Because she was beautiful, and I had no reason to reject her; my mother would have killed me."

Nikhil, offering his perspective, remarked, "You're right about your mother killing you. You made a big mistake. All you had to do was get to know her, and then if you liked her, you would have automatically fallen in love. But you never gave it a chance."

Samrat brushed it off, saying, "Relax, I'll find someone better, and then I'll show you guys."

Vedant, teasingly, responded, "You are going to die alone."

Samrat, confidently, retorted, "When I fall in love, I'll let you know, but you two are not invited to my wedding."

Nikhil, with a mischievous tone, asked, "Tell me something, will you be serving food at your own wedding?"

Vedant burst into laughter and added, "Oh, we are coming to your wedding no matter what. We want to see you serve food."

Nikhil continued the banter, saying, "Can I have some more chicken, chef?" They all laughed out loud, and even though Samrat tried to keep a straight face, he couldn't help but smile, finding the situation amusing as well.

They took turns driving, and after hours on the road, they finally reached Goa at 1:40 in the night. They had booked a private villa situated on a small hillside. This villa was part of a collection built by a club resort called The Tree House Villa Hotel. The resort's lobby, party hall, clubhouse, gym, and a vast garden were located below, while the individual villas were perched up the hill. Despite their proximity, the villas were strategically spaced, ensuring privacy for each. Every villa boasted a private swimming pool and a fireplace in the front yard.

Upon arrival, they entered the lobby, where the receptionist warmly greeted them. After completing the necessary check-in procedures, the receptionist called Manohar, their service manager. Manohar guided them and led them to their villa atop the hill, it was a walkable distance and took less than five minutes.

Arriving at their destination, they were greeted by a stunning triangular-shaped villa. It appeared as though the roof touched the ground, with a glass facade on the front, offering a glimpse of the interior bathed in yellow lights. The villa glowed, creating a warm and inviting ambiance. Outside, the porch was adorned with chairs, surrounded by the beauty of trees, enhancing the charm of this uniquely shaped abode.

Their service manager, Manohar, led them inside and remarked, "Sir, it is late, or else I would have given you a tour of this place. But no worries, Sir, I'll do that in the morning. I am sure you must have been tired of all that traveling. Let me show you the bath."

Manohar guided them to a spacious bathroom featuring a large Jacuzzi. He demonstrated how it worked and suggested, "Sir, why don't you relax and get fresh, while I'll arrange your dinner for tonight."

Nikhil tipped Manohar and thanked him for his assistance. Samrat, Nikhil, and Vedant, without bothering to unpack their suitcases, stripped down and immersed themselves in the hot tub.

All three were so exhausted that they savored the hot, churning water, indulging in a relaxing soak for 30 minutes. The tub was spacious enough for the trio.

After emerging, clad in fluffy white bathrobes, they found a spread laid out on the table.

Manohar assured them, "The housekeeping staff will clear when you're finished. I'll be here by noon. Thank you, Sir." Manohar left, leaving them to enjoy their meal.

Vedant, Samrat, and Nikhil were so famished that they quickly devoured their food. After the hearty meal, they headed upstairs to inspect their room. A massive king-size bed awaited them, and the three of them collapsed onto its soft surface. As soon as they hit the bed, they drifted into a deep, well-deserved sleep.

Day 1: Friday,

The next morning, sunlight gently streamed into their room, rousing them from their sleep. Vedant, not quite ready to face the day, buried his face in a pillow. Samrat and Nikhil, drawn to the glass window, were greeted by a breathtaking sight. The day was beautiful, with a private swimming pool in the front, a small mountain in the background, and lush greenery everywhere.

Samrat and Nikhil exchanged glances, excitement written all over their faces. They hurriedly rummaged through their bags, searching for their swimming trunks.

All the commotion eventually woke Vedant, who groggily inquired, "What the hell are you guys searching for?" Nikhil found his trunk and showed it to Vedant, who promptly entered the bathroom to change, while Samrat continued his search.

Lethargically, Vedant got up from his bed and ambled over to the window. Samrat triumphantly yelled, "Found it!" and rushed into the bathroom. Witnessing the scenic beauty outside, his moment lasted for a short while when he could see Samrat and Nikhil running towards the pool and making a splashing jump to the refreshing waters.

He couldn't resist the allure and hurriedly made his way to his bag. A few minutes later, Samrat and Nikhil saw Vedant running towards them, culminating in a dramatic splash into the pool.

After some playful moments in the pool, a hotel staff member approached and asked if they would like to have breakfast outside.

Vedant inquired, "Where will we eat?" The hotel staff pointed to a place next to the villa. A white-colored wooden picnic table with attached benches stood under a shady tree.

Following their refreshing pool time, the trio headed for a hearty breakfast, enjoying the spread laid out for them on the picnic table.

After breakfast, the boys headed back to the villa to freshen up. They unpacked their bags, stowed their belongings in the wardrobe, changed into something comfortable, and headed out. As they reached the door, they encountered Manohar.

Manohar greeted them, "If you have not made any plans, may I show you around our Tree House Villa Hotel?"

Nikhil replied, "Yes, why not?" So Manohar, their service manager, took them on a tour of the club resort, showcasing its various amenities.

After exploring the entire place, they arrived at another end of the resort, where a river flowed below. Manohar suggested, "If you love fishing, we can arrange for a boat. While fishing, you can enjoy drinks as well, and the price for the boat ride will be on an hourly basis, including fishing rods and drinks."

Vedant eagerly proposed, "Let's give it a try."

Samrat, practical as always, inquired, "What about the fish we catch?"

Manohar chuckled, "Easy said than done. If you do catch any fish, I'll prepare a grilled barbecue for lunch, and our chef will take care of your catch."

Nikhil nodded in agreement, saying, "Sounds nice."

Eventually, they hopped onto a local, colorful, small fishing boat with a driver's cabin. Three chairs and fishing rods were attached to the front deck of the boat.

The boat had just one person, the captain, who would navigate and occasionally guide them in using the fishing rods.

A bucket full of ice with beer cans stuffed in it completed the setup. The weather was perfect, a cool and sunny day. Nikhil, Samrat, and Vedant relaxed in their chairs, each with a beer can in hand, eagerly awaiting a catch.

The boat drifted to the middle of the river, bringing about a sense of peace. The boys, soaking in the moment, felt like they were having the best day of their lives.

Time flew by unnoticed, and before they knew it, an hour had passed. Though they hadn't caught anything yet, they were thoroughly enjoying the boat ride.

The boat captain announced, "In five minutes, we will be heading back to the shore."

Just then, Samrat got a bite. He yelled, "Help! Help!" Nikhil and Vedant leaped from their chairs to assist Samrat in pulling the fish up. It was a struggle, but the fish eventually surfaced. The boat captain skillfully used a fish net scoop to trap the fish.

He exclaimed, "Wow, it's a foot-long Surmai (Kingfish). This river has smaller fish, and they are difficult to catch. You're lucky to catch this stray one."

Samrat stood proudly on the boat, holding the fish by its tail and a fishing rod in the other hand, while Nikhil and Vedant stood beside him. The boat captain, capturing the moment, took a picture on their phone.

Back at the villa, when Manohar saw their catch, he was surprised and exclaimed, "You caught this?"

Samrat proudly affirmed, "Yes." Manohar, still in disbelief, commented, "That's impossible. You are one lucky fisherman."

At lunch, a table was set next to the pool, and true to the promise, the hotel chef cleaned and prepped the fish.

The chef marveled, "What a catch! No fish beats its smooth and succulent, fleshy texture, especially when cooked fresh. It easily takes in the spices and can be treated in any form. I would suggest shallow-fried fish steaks. What do you think?"

Vedant eagerly responded, "What are you waiting for? Go ahead."

Vedant, Nikhil, and Samrat savored their afternoon lunch when Manohar showed up again. Manohar inquired, "I hope you enjoyed the lunch, and how was the fish prepared?"

Nikhil complimented, "Everything was great, and the fish was excellent."

Vedant asked Manohar, "Can we climb up the mountain?" pointing at the small mountain opposite the pool.

Samrat chimed in, "Yeah, something like hiking and stuff."

Manohar explained, "It's not that high for hiking, but we do set up camp for our guests on the top. The view is awesome – on one side, you can see our villas glow in the dark, and on the other side, there's a long beach. It looks as if the beach is near, but it's quite far from here."

Curious, Samrat asked, "What about the tent and the camping gear?"

Manohar assured them, "Everything will be arranged. Three comfortable large tents, each accommodating two people easily. Food will be provided in tiffins, there will be sleeping bags, a fire lighter for a campfire, and a radio for music. It will be dark and spooky, windy, with an open sky, a bonfire, and a perfect setup."

Excited, Samrat turned to the group, asking, "Guys, what do you think?"

Vedant agreed, "I guess we should experience this as well."

Nikhil inquired, "When can you arrange this camp?"

Manohar suggested, "How about tomorrow late in the evening? You spend the night there, and we'll come back in the morning to get you back to your villa."

Samrat approved, "Sounds cool."

Nikhil, however, wondered, "But then, why not tonight?"

Manohar explained, "The reason being, that there is a party arranged by our club at the party hall. It's a costume party, and people from outside the club are also invited, so there will be a good lively crowd."

Nikhil asked, "Where can we get a costume?" Manohar provided them with an address to a shop where they could buy costumes.

Later in the evening, the guys decided to explore the market. They rented three scooters and drove off to the local streets of Goa. After quite a bit of shopping in the local market, they eventually found the costume shop.

Vedant shopped on his own, while Nikhil and Samrat were struggling.

After a little while, Samrat emerged wearing a costume - a thin, sleeveless red vest jacket, a yellow straw hat with a red band, and rolled-up jeans till his knees.

Nikhil looked at him and asked, "And who are you supposed to be?"

Samrat proudly proclaimed, "The fellow at the counter said this is trending now. It belongs to a character named Monkey D. Luffy, and he said only one piece left."

Nikhil, with a smirk, remarked, "You mean... last piece left."

Samrat, after a moment of thought, replied, "No, I am sure he said one piece left." He then pulled out a white T-shirt and offered it to Nikhil, saying, "Here, I got you a T-shirt."

Samrat added, "Hope it's the right size."

Nikhil examined the T-shirt, revealing the same character with 'One-Piece' written on it. Reading it aloud, Nikhil said, "One-Piece."

Samrat explained, "Huh... No, they had many. It was piled up. I just picked one. Hope it fits you fine."

Nikhil, unimpressed, retorted, "I am supposed to wear a costume, not a T-shirt."

Samrat insisted, "But I want you to wear this T-shirt. In case nobody recognizes my costume, I can show them your T-shirt print and say I am playing this character."

In frustration, Nikhil threw the T-shirt on Samrat's face.

Vedant showed up with a frizzy long hair wig, a T-shirt with 'Hellfire Club' printed on it, and a fake guitar.

Nikhil asked Vedant, "And you are?"

Vedant replied, "Eddie Munson from Stranger Things."

Vedant then looked at Samrat and remarked, "One-Piece?"

Samrat proudly affirmed, "Yes, and I got the last one."

Vedant sighed, "Oh God, One-Piece is a Japanese manga series, and the protagonist is Monkey D. Luffy."

Nikhil intervened, "Forget this moron and help me find a costume."

A few minutes later, Vedant and Samrat were waiting outside, and that's when Nikhil showed up.

Samrat, looking at him, asked, "Why is he wearing a helmet?"

Vedant explained, "He's dressed as a Mandalorian."

Nikhil, curious, asked Vedant, "Is this a Star Wars thing?"

Vedant confirmed, "Yes, and remember your punch line is 'This is the way.'"

Nikhil repeated, "This is the way."

Vedant added, "Right."

Nikhil then asked, "Why am I carrying this green gremlin soft toy?"

Vedant smacked his head and said, "It's not a gremlin; it's a baby Yoda and it's called Grogu."

So finally, all three of them were ready for the costume party.

Later in the evening at the party, the crowd was amazing, and the DJ played awesome tracks. Everyone was in a costume, with several Monkey D. Luffy costumes on the floor. Samrat humorously remarked, "Now I know why only one piece was left."

The most popular costume was the Mandalorian, and Nikhil enjoyed all the attention. All three of them had a blast at the party, which ran late into the night.

Day 2: Saturday

The next day, the boys woke up way past noon. The hangover from the previous night was hitting them hard. They decided to order some coffee and a light breakfast to ease the pain. Seeking relief, they took turns relaxing in the Jacuzzi, hoping to shake off the remnants of the wild night.

Fully refreshed, Nikhil, Samrat, and Vedant decided it was time for some adventure. They opted to rent scooters again for the day.

Their first mission – find a local spot for lunch. After navigating through a maze of small alleys, they stumbled upon a charming local restaurant serving authentic Goan home-cooked meals. The place was packed, but the determined trio managed to secure a table.

The menu was simple yet inviting. Without hesitation, the boys ordered the regular seafood thali. When the food arrived, it was nothing short of heavenly – fried fish, crab curry, clam curry, prawn stir fry, rice, and solkadhi.

Solkadhi, a pink-colored drink made with coconut milk, salt, chilli-garlic paste, and green chillies mixed with kokum, added the perfect tang to the feast. Each sip left a lasting impression.

Satisfied and energized, the boys decided to explore the local culture. They headed to a nearby church, absorbing the serenity of the place.

Later, they made their way to the beach, intending to unwind. However, they were met with the excitement of water sports activities.

Nikhil, Samrat, and Vedant couldn't resist the temptation and ended up indulging in parasailing and scuba diving, creating unforgettable memories.

As the sun began its descent, they returned to the beach, soaking in the peaceful ambiance until the sky painted hues of orange and pink.

It was a day filled with laughter, delicious food, and thrilling adventures – the kind of day that lingers in memory long after the sun has set.

Later, when they reached the villa, Manohar was waiting for them. Vedant inquired, "What is it, Manohar? Were you waiting for us?"

Manohar replied, "Sir, I told you I'd arrange camping on top of the mountain."

Vedant said, "Oh yeah, we forgot all about it."

Nikhil chimed in, "What about dinner?"

Manohar assured them, "Like I said, we have arranged tiffins for you."

Nikhil suggested, "Might as well spend a night in the camp." Manohar added, "Better wear double T-shirts; it gets chilly up there."

After a quick change, Manohar and a hotel staff member guided the boys to the hill's summit. It was a 40-minute climb to the top.

Upon arrival, three camping tents were already set up on the flat camping ground. Inside the tents, sleeping bags awaited them.

The hotel staff lit a bonfire and tuned a radio, which unfortunately started playing back-to-back ads after a single song.

Manohar had arranged a short, foldable table where he placed the tiffin boxes. He also brought an icebox filled with beer cans and a 10-liter water dispenser with a tap below, he said, "Enjoy your camping. Usually, there are more campers here, but today it will only be you guys. There's nothing to be scared of; there are no wild animals or any animals, for that matter. But in case you decide to come back to your villa, just give me a call, and my guys will come to take you below."

Vedant reassured, "Don't worry about us; we'll have a good time here."

Nikhil added, "Yeah, it's pitch dark around here, but I think we'll manage."

Samrat, feeling hungry, declared, "I am hungry; let's eat."

Manohar concluded, "Okay, sir. I'll be back in the morning by 8 AM. Enjoy your stay and have fun." With that, Manohar and his hotel staff hiked back down the mountain.

The radio played old Konkani songs, the hotel staff must have tuned it to the local channel. Nikhil, Vedant, and Samrat strolled to the edge of the cliff. Though it was dark, the moonlight allowed them to faintly see the beach in the distance. They then walked to another end of the cliff, and the whole resort was visible due to the lights, creating a beautiful view.

They settled down for dinner and cracked open their beer cans. Having their meal close to the bonfire, they listened to the local Konkani songs playing on the radio. The rhythmic tunes added to the ambiance, creating a perfect setting for a night spent under the stars.

Later, after dinner, they sat next to the fire and chatted for a while. Soon, the conversation slowly veered toward haunting stories, as the ambiance and surroundings practically begged for it.

Vedant kicked things off by sharing his spooky experience. Then, Samrat contributed a mild scary story. After he finished, both of them turned their eyes to Nikhil.

Vedant asked Nikhil, "Don't you have a scary story to tell?"

Nikhil hesitated, saying, "I do... but I think let's not push this. We're practically alone here in this dark place."

Vedant insisted, "Come on, we're not scared. Tell us your story." So, Nikhil reluctantly said, "Okay... I don't know if this will scare you or not, but it's a real story that happened in 1959. A group of Russian hikers, all young like us, disappeared in the remote Ural Mountains in western Siberia. They abandoned their tent hours after settling down, and they disappeared."

Vedant and Samrat looked at each other, then glanced around their surroundings, but Nikhil didn't stop he continued.

"Weeks later, investigators found their tent. It was cut from the inside. Their bodies were found 1500 meters away from their tent, frozen to death. They were barefoot and in their sleeping clothes. What made them run barefoot on the ice this far...?"

Nikhil's storytelling took a darker turn, and it grew scarier and longer. He delved into the possibilities of aliens, UFOs, and even an

Abominable Snowman. As he spoke, the eerie surroundings seemed to match the mood of his tale.

The tale became too much for Samrat, who said, "I think we won't be able to sleep tonight if you carry on."

Nikhil agreed, saying, "I guess you're right, and I'm not sleeping alone. The tent is big enough for two. I think, Samrat, we should sleep together."

The night settled around them, shrouded in both the chilling tale and the dark silence of the wilderness.

Vedant chuckled, "Both of you are scaredy-cats. I guess it's getting late; we should get into our tents."

Finally, they decided to call it a night, and they were in no mood to hear the rest of the story. Nikhil and Samrat chose to sleep together, while Vedant, unafraid, went to sleep alone in his tent.

About half an hour later, Samrat woke Nikhil. Nikhil, who was deep in sleep, opened his eyes and looked at Samrat. Samrat whispered, "There's something outside our tent."

Nikhil, struggling to free himself from his sleeping bag, noticed a shadow moving around the tent. Anxiety started to wash over Nikhil, and Samrat, frozen in fear, whispered again, "Do you have a knife?" Nikhil, confused, mumbled, "Huh...?" The shadow drew closer and pulled the tent zippers open.

Nikhil and Samrat let out screams that could wake up the entire forest. They were terrified for their lives. However, it was Vedant. He understood they were scared and calmly stated, "It's me."

Samrat, still agitated, yelled back at Vedant, "Why are you scaring us?" Nikhil saw Vedant carrying his sleeping bag and realized what had happened. He tapped Samrat and said, "He's not scaring us; he himself is a scaredy-cat."

Without wasting any time, Vedant entered the tent, and all three of them managed to squeeze into it for the night. The dark wilderness surrounding them became the backdrop for an unexpected sleepover, thanks to Vedant's attempt to conquer his own fears.

Day 3: Sunday

The next morning, at sharp 8 AM, the hotel staff arrived. He got worried when he saw two tents empty. With a furrowed brow, he approached the third tent and pulled the zipper open. To his surprise, he found Nikhil, Samrat, and Vedant all squeezed into one tent. They had just woken up and were sitting there, looking embarrassed as the hotel staff stared at them. Without wasting any time, they scrambled out of the tent.

The hotel staff informed them that he had brought breakfast and insisted they enjoy it there. So, they sat at the edge of the cliff, with the perfect breeze and an awesome view of the distant beach. While they savored their breakfast, the hotel staff efficiently started winding up the campsite.

After the mountain breakfast, they descended to the villa. They freshened up and spent some leisure time in the villa. They watched TV, mixed some drinks, and basked in the comfort of the villa. Just as they were settling in, Samrat's phone rang. It was a call from home. Samrat noticed a small balcony in the corner and decided to take his drink and his call out there.

It was his Mom on the other end, and she delivered some bad news. "Beta, there is a bad news. The girl you met before leaving has rejected the proposal," she said.

Samrat responded with a simple "Oh." His Mom continued, "Yeah, it is disappointing because she was very good-looking and well-mannered. It's a big miss."

Trying to console his mother, Samrat said, "It's okay, Mom. I'll find a better girl soon." His Mom, however, had a different perspective. "She was in the better category, and if she has rejected you, then I think what you should be saying is, 'I'll find a girl soon.' Don't search for better or good, just search for a girl."

Samrat, feeling a bit agitated, muttered, "Mom!" She quickly apologized, "Sorry, I am sounding mean, but I am disappointed that she didn't even give you a chance. If she would have, she would have known what a wonderful person you are."

After his conversation with his Mom, Samrat was overcome with a sinking feeling. Sadness enveloped him as he thought, 'Mom doesn't know that it's not her, but it's me who has not given her a chance. If I did, I would have gotten to know her more, and maybe I would have liked her. Even my friends think the same. I think I made a blunder here.'

Samrat's mood took a downturn after the call. Meanwhile, Manohar appeared at the door, and Vedant welcomed him in.

Manohar announced, "We have organized a Goan food festival below at the club, so I have come to give you these food coupons. For our guests, everything is free. Just hand over these coupons, and you can eat at any stall below. Hope you enjoy your afternoon meal." Saying this, Manohar handed over a bunch of coupons to the guys and left.

The gang headed to the food festival for lunch. Samrat was unusually quiet, and both Nikhil and Vedant noticed.

Concerned, Vedant asked Samrat, "Is everything okay? You seem a bit upset." Samrat just smiled and remained silent.

Upon reaching the food festival venue, they found a decent crowd. Various stalls showcasing local Goan food were on display under a huge tent, there were tables and chairs and they were neatly arranged at the center of the tent. Nikhil and Vedant instructed Samrat to secure a table while they went to get the food. They used the coupons to gather enough food and returned to the table.

Samrat, however, seemed to have lost his appetite.

Nikhil asked him, "What's wrong? Is everything okay?"

Samrat looked at him, took a breath, and after a pause, he said, "You guys were right."

Vedant inquired, "Right about?"

Samrat admitted, "Varsha, I think I made a mistake."

Nikhil reassured him, "You worry too much; it's not like she'll get married to someone else the next day. You can still contact her and talk to her; I am sure she will understand."

This statement brought a smile to Samrat's face, and his mood lightened. Vedant, trying to shift the focus, said, "Try this, it's delicious." Finally, they started enjoying the meal spread out on the table, which had four chairs—one of them conspicuously vacant.

A guy approached them and said, "Hi, can I join you guys if you don't mind?"

Vedant replied, "No problem, man. Have a seat."

So the guy joined them, bringing his plate of food along. He introduced himself, saying, "Hi, I am Praful."

The guys reciprocated with their introductions. Soon, they delved into a conversation and discovered that Praful worked for an event organization company.

Praful remarked, "So today is the last day of your vacation."

Samrat affirmed, "Yes, we will check out tomorrow early morning."

Praful inquired, "Early morning as in?"

Nikhil specified, "4 AM."

After a brief pause, Praful suggested, "If you don't mind, can I suggest something?"

Vedant asked, "What is it?"

Praful explained, "There is a forest party – live band, food, drinks, and the works. The party starts at 8 in the evening and will go on until 4 AM." Nikhil, naturally suspicious, queried, "What's the catch?"

Praful clarified, "Well, you see, I work there. I'll be leaving now after lunch, and my work will be finished by 3 AM. I need to leave for Mumbai by 3 AM. So, what I want is a free ride home, and in return, I'll give you three passes to this party. These passes are difficult to get and are expensive. You can come by 7.30 and park the car in the staff area. I'll give you a parking sticker. Then, you can enjoy the party and have as many drinks as you want. Since I don't drink, I'll drive for you. But please be back at the parking area at 3.00 AM sharp. So, what do you think? You'll only be leaving an hour early, and I'll do all the driving."

Vedant replied, "Sounds good, but first can I see your ID card and your driver's license?"

Praful swiftly produced both cards. Vedant took pictures of them and then captured Praful's image, sending all three to his dad.

Puzzled, Praful asked, "What are you doing?"

Vedant explained, "I sent these pictures to my Dad. No offense, just being on the safe side."

Praful understandingly said, "No issue. I can understand your concern, but trust me, I am just a middle-class working guy."

Nikhil intervened, "Okay, deal. We'll be there by 7.30 in the evening." Praful handed them the passes and the parking sticker. They exchanged phone numbers, and Praful thanked them for their help before leaving.

After lunch, the boys decided to spend their last day on the beach. Samrat, Nikhil, and Vedant took a refreshing swim. The water was just right, and after some fun in the waves, they lounged on the beach.

Approaching 5 PM, Nikhil suggested, "If we have to reach there by 7.30 or 8.00, then we should leave now. We have to freshen up, pack our bags, and then check out; it will take time."

Samrat sighed, "I can't believe this is our last day in Goa."

Vedant reassured him, "Don't be sad; we are lucky to get those great passes. Let's party hard like it's our last day in Goa."

Nikhil added, "It is our last day in Goa."

Vedant grinned, "I know, let's go have a blast." So, they decided to leave the beach and head towards the hotel.

Finally, at 6.30, they were at the lobby for checkout, and Manohar was there to assist. Manohar said, "Sir, I hope you liked this place and enjoyed your stay."

Vedant replied, "The place was awesome, and we are going to recommend this place to our friends and family." Manohar was delighted and thanked them, helping them to their car. Vedant tipped him well.

After an hour's drive, they reached their destination. They called Praful from their phone and parked their SUV at the staff parking area. Praful was glad to see them.

Nikhil asked, "What if anyone asks us to take our car out of here?"

Praful assured, "I gave you a car parking sticker; just stick it on the glass."

Samrat affixed the staff parking sticker. Praful reminded them, "So, enjoy your party, but don't be late. Be here at sharp 3.00 AM, okay?"

Nikhil affirmed, "Don't worry, we'll be here by 3."

And so, the party was on. It was an open area with lots of tall trees around. The crowd was sensational, with a live band playing loud music, laser lights, an open bar, and food counters.

Vedant, Samrat, and Nikhil first had a couple of drinks. Then, armed with beer cans, they danced the moment they entered the scene.

After a couple of hours, they got tired, so they grabbed some food from the counters, sat under a tree, and had their meal. Once they were full, they grabbed more beer cans and disappeared into the dancing crowd.

Several hours later, Nikhil checked the time; it was 2:40, and Vedant and Samrat were missing in the crowd. Though a little tipsy, Nikhil started looking for his friends. As he searched, a hand fell on his shoulders, and when he turned around, it was Vedant.

Vedant said, "Dude, where have you been? I've been looking for you. Have you seen the time?"

Nikhil asked, "Where is Samrat?"

Vedant, also a little drunk, replied, "Let's find him."

Five minutes later, they found Samrat at the food counter, devouring a burger. Nikhil and Vedant called out together, "Samrat!" Startled, Samrat looked behind, holding the half-eaten burger. Samrat said, "Guys, where were you? Do you know the time? It's almost 3 o'clock."

It was 2:55 when they reached the parking area. Praful was already standing there with his backpack.

Praful said, "Wow, I am impressed. I left 5 minutes early because I thought I'd have to search for you in the crowd." Nobody was in a position to say anything; they just entered the car and fell asleep.

Praful woke Vedant up and said, "I need the keys."

Vedant searched for them, then pulled them out of his pocket and handed them over to Praful. All three of them fell asleep in the back, and Praful took the car, heading off to Mumbai.

TWO

LOVE RESET.

It was Monday, and when the boys woke up, it was already afternoon. Praful, still behind the wheel, had been driving for a solid 11 hours. The guys groaned, nursing hangovers as Praful pulled over next to a bustling Chinese stall.

Nikhil groaned, "How far have we come?"

Praful grinned, "Just a couple more hours. We're almost there."

Vedant, concerned, chimed in, "You didn't take a break; you must be tired."

Praful chuckled, "Stopped for tea twice, but you guys were in dreamland."

They ordered spicy manchow soup, hoping to shake off their hangovers.

Samrat sighed, "Three days gone, just like that."

Reality hit them – the vacation was over, and the normalization had kicked in.

Nikhil mumbled, "Back to reality, guys."

Praful laughed, "Wind up, we just have a couple more hours of driving."

Vedant offered, "I'll take the wheel; you must be tired."

Praful agreed, and they shuffled into the car, Praful settled in behind, next to Samrat, while Nikhil took the front seat beside Vedant, who took charge of the wheels.

An hour into their journey, traffic began to build up, a sure sign that their destination was drawing near.

Vedant, turning to Praful, suggested, "I can drop you at your place."

Praful declined, "No need, my brother's picking me up."

Samrat chimed in, "The party was awesome, thanks for the passes."

Praful replied, "Your welcome, but you guys have done me a favor, by giving me a ride home. By the way, who's Varsha?"

Samrat was stunned; words eluded him. Nikhil spun around, asking, "How do you know Varsha?" Pointing at Samrat, Praful grinned, "Well, he kept saying 'I love you, Varsha.'"

A moment of silence hung in the air, and then Vedant and Nikhil looked at each other and burst into laughter. The tension dissolved, and they found themselves harmonizing with a classic Hindi romantic song, 'Yeh Jo Mohabbat Hai' from the movie 'Kati Patang'. Their laughter seamlessly blended with the melody.

Praful realized he shouldn't have brought it up; he cast a slow glance at Samrat, who was now flushed with embarrassment. Praful, sensing the need to break the awkwardness, requested Vedant to pull over. Vedant skillfully maneuvered the car to a stop.

As Praful stepped out, he remarked, "My brother will pick me up from here. Thanks for the ride." With a quick farewell, Praful walked away.

Samrat remained unusually quiet, Vedant and Nikhil, sensing the tension, decided to lift the spirits.

Vedant halted the car near a Vadapav cart, suggesting, "I'm hungry. Let's grab a quick bite." While munching on Vadapav, Nikhil, attempting to ease the atmosphere, said to Samrat, "I have an idea. Why don't you get her address from your mom, and we can go pay her a visit?"

Samrat looked at Nikhil, disbelief in his eyes, and retorted, "Are you crazy? What will I tell my mom if she asks why I need her address?"

Vedant chimed in, "Do you have her number?"

Samrat admitted, "Yes."

Nikhil, with a mischievous grin, questioned, "How did you get her number?"

Samrat explained, "My mom messaged me when I left."

Vedant took the number and dialed it on his phone. Samrat, puzzled, asked Nikhil, "What is he doing?" On the other end of the line, Varsha answered, "Hello?" Vedant, putting on a casual tone, said, "Madam, I'm from the courier company. Samrat has sent you a souvenir from Goa, but we seem to have misplaced your address. Unfortunately, we're unable to reach Samrat as well. Could you please provide your address so that we can ensure the safe delivery of the gift?" Vedant deftly borrowed Nikhil's phone to note down the address.

"Here's the address, easy-peasy," Vedant declared.

Samrat, slightly flustered, muttered, "Why did you do that? Now I have to send her a gift."

Nikhil, grinning, retorted, "You are the gift, dummy. We're heading to her place right now." Vedant, checking the address, added, "And it's not far from here. Let's get in the car."

After an hour's drive, they arrived in Mumbai, and their first stop was Varsha's house. Varsha resided in a modest three-floor building, her flat conveniently located on the ground floor. The entrance to her apartment was visible from the building's gate.

Nikhil nudged Samrat, saying, "Go ring the bell."

Samrat hesitated, expressing nervousness.

Vedant teased, "Come on, you were confident enough to tell her you don't prefer arranged marriage, and now you're scared to admit you're in love."

Samrat admitted, "Yes."

Nikhil proposed, "Okay, we'll both come with you, but we'll stand behind at a distance."

The trio approached the door, and Samrat rang the bell. After a few anxious moments, Varsha opened the door, elegantly dressed. Samrat stood in awe, taking in her appearance.

Varsha, surprised to see him, said, "Samrat?" He stammered, "Hi, Varsha. I was just passing by, and I thought..."

Just then, Vinod entered from inside, also dressed sharply in formal. Varsha, sensing the situation, wasted no time and said, "Meet Vinod, we are seeing each other." Vinod, easy-going, approached with a warm smile, shaking Samrat's hand. He then glanced behind and greeted Vedant and Nikhil.

Vedant whispered to Nikhil, "She didn't waste time finding herself another guy."

Nikhil chuckled, "Look at her; guys must have lined up for her. All she had to do was swipe right."

Varsha turned to Samrat and asked, "Is there anything you wanted to say? Actually, we are going out on a date."

Samrat caught off guard, stammered, "Oh, I just... um... yeah. I wanted to know if you could give me some guitar lessons, but never mind. I'll come later or I'll just text you."

Varsha, surprised by Samrat's unexpected request, decided not to make a big deal out of it. She simply replied, "Okay," and then took Vinod's arm, walking past Samrat.

In a gentle voice, Vinod said, "I didn't know you played the guitar." Varsha nervously smiled and replied in a lower voice, "Neither did I."

Samrat stood there, glancing at Nikhil and Vedant. Soon, they found themselves back in the car.

Vedant remarked, "Guitar lessons, really?"

Samrat shrugged, "I couldn't think of anything else."

Nikhil couldn't contain himself and burst into laughter. Vedant, slowly turning back, exchanged a look with Samrat, and they all erupted into laughter.

Eventually, Vedant dropped Nikhil and Samrat at their place. Then, he headed straight home. Amidst all the drama, Vedant had completely forgotten about Malavika. He had committed to helping her unpack and even bringing along his friends for assistance. However, Vedant, lost in the day's events, went straight home. After freshening up and having an early dinner, he felt weary enough to retire for the night.

When Samrat arrived home, his mom noticed the unhappiness etched on his face. After a quick shower, he returned to find his mom brewing him a cup of coffee. While preparing it, she gently inquired, "Is everything okay? You seemed a little upset. Did you have a bad time in Goa?"

Samrat managed a smile and reassured her, "No, Mom, Goa was great. I'll show you the pictures I took with my phone later." She handed him the coffee mug and went back to her chores.

Samrat, holding the warm mug, retreated to the balcony. Despite his attempt to brush off the question, his mind lingered on Varsha.

Meanwhile, Nikhil reached his place. He took the lift and strolled onto his floor. The building exuded an eerie silence. Nikhil fumbled for his keys, unlocked the door, and entered. A sudden gust of cold air smacked him in the face. To his shock, the room was not as he left it.

Four girls, clad in their pajamas, lay sprawled across the room. Perplexed, Nikhil squinted at the nameplate on the door, wondering if he had mistakenly entered the wrong flat. His gaze settled on Priya among the slumbering quartet. They all seemed to be in a deep sleep, undisturbed by his intrusion.

The television droned on at a low volume, casting a dim glow on the room. The air conditioner hummed, leaving the entire place chilled to the core. Empty beer bottles and pizza boxes are scattered about, indicating a recent party. Nikhil stood in confusion, trying to make sense of the unexpected scene.

Reluctant to disturb the sleeping girls, clad in their nightwear, Nikhil tiptoed around the room. He made his way to the TV, switching it off quietly. Next, he turned off the air conditioner, opting for the gentler whir of the ceiling fan. With a final glance at the unexpected guests, Nikhil decided to step outside.

Closing the door behind him, he sat down with his bag beside him. He hoped that the girls wouldn't sleep the night away, anticipating the moment when they would awaken to the curious situation.

As darkness enveloped the corridor, Nikhil pondered that the beer must have taken its toll, lulling the girls into a deep sleep. Concerned about his friend Samrat, he decided to check in on him. Dialing Samrat's number, they engaged in a conversation.

Samrat, reflective, admitted, "I made a mistake by not giving Varsha a chance."

Encouragingly, Nikhil responded, "Don't give up. She's just dating someone. You still have a chance. Why don't you start texting her? Send her light messages and see what kind of response she gives."

Samrat, finding merit in the idea, agreed to give it a try. The conversation then shifted to Nikhil's own romantic complications.

Samrat inquired "What about your teenage girlfriend?" prompting him to share his story.

After hearing Nikhil's situation, Samrat, taken aback, exclaimed, "Are you crazy? Wake them up and call the police. They should be in jail."

Nikhil, with a shrug, retorted, "Dude, she has my scooter keys, and besides, I am never good at creating a scene. It's best I wait."

Samrat, concerned for his friend, suggested, "Come over to my place and go back in the morning."

Nikhil, determined to stay put, replied, "No, I'll wait here."

Samrat, respecting Nikhil's decision, said, "Okay, do what suits you. Call me if you need anything." The two friends ended the call, leaving Nikhil alone with his thoughts in the building corridor next to his door.

After his conversation with Samrat, Nikhil's mind replayed Priya's words about being a vlogger. Curiosity getting the better of him, he decided to delve into her social media profile. Scrolling through her posts, he stumbled upon her latest vlog, which revolved around her Pajama Party.

In the video, Priya shared her initial plans for the party, detailing the excitement and preparations. However, fate had different ideas, and the party got canceled due to unexpected guests at her friend's house, where the event was supposed to unfold. Undeterred, Priya, ever the spontaneous one, hatched a new plan.

She decided to sneak into her neighbor's house, keys in hand, taking advantage of her neighbor's absence, who was out on a holiday.

In the video, she animatedly narrated how she called her three friends over, informed her mom she was off to a Pajama Party at a friend's place, and, in reality, stealthily entered the vacant neighbor's home.

Once inside, the girls wasted no time in making themselves at home. They cranked up the air conditioner to create a cool atmosphere, setting the stage for their makeshift party. Music filled the air, and the room came alive with their laughter and dance.

Meanwhile, in her own house, Priya's mother caught a faint echo of music wafting in from the neighboring apartment. However, dismissing it as inconsequential, she chose to ignore the distant sounds.

Unbeknownst to her, Priya continued to document every moment of their impromptu gathering. The girls, resourceful as ever, managed to procure beer and generously stocked Nikhil's fridge. The atmosphere was set for an unforgettable night as they ordered copious amounts of pizza, filling the room with laughter, chatter, and the clinking of bottles.

The video captured the essence of their carefree party as they indulged in eating, drinking, and dancing to their heart's content. The revelry continued into the wee hours, creating a lively spectacle within the walls of Nikhil's apartment.

Meanwhile, back at Nikhil's end, he watched the unfolding events on the video. As the night wore on, fatigue took its toll on him, and he eventually fell asleep.

The clock struck 3:00 AM, and Vedant abruptly awoke from his bed, as though jolted by a haunting nightmare. Yet, his nightmare wasn't one of ghosts or monsters; it was the realization of a promise he had made to Malavika. Regret and a sense of duty spurred him into action.

Quietly, he slipped out of bed, dressed hastily, muttering to himself, "How could I forget such a thing?" With a determined yet silent resolve, Vedant maneuvered his motorcycle onto the main road. Keeping a discreet distance, he kick-started the engine, ensuring that the noise wouldn't reach the ears of anyone back home who might question his midnight venture.

Upon reaching Malavika's residence, he observed that her door remained securely locked. Parking his motorcycle to the side, Vedant settled onto the porch, patiently waiting. Fatigue from the disrupted night weighed on him, and he found solace in the quiet darkness as he waited for Malavika to come. Soon, the weariness caught up with him, and he dozed off, his unfinished sleep claiming its due.

It was a bright and sunny Tuesday morning. Priya's mother stepped out of her flat to soak in the warm sunlight that bathed her corridor. As she enjoyed the rays, her gaze landed on Nikhil, who was still slumbering outside his door. A sense of surprise overcame her, and she hurried over to wake him.

Nikhil, deep in his sleep, woke up with a befuddled expression as Priya's mother inquired, "Did you lose your keys?"

Nikhil, in a rush, got up and replied, "No, I have my keys with me."

Perplexed, Priya's mother questioned, "Then why are you still outside, and why were you sleeping next to your door?"

Nikhil explained, "I couldn't open the door with my keys, so I slept outside. I thought I would ask for the spare key from you in the morning."

Observing Nikhil's struggle, Priya's mother suggested, "Show me the key, let me try."

However, Nikhil hesitated and pretended to search for the key. "I can't seem to find it," he claimed.

Suspicion crept in as Priya's mother probed, "Why are you acting strange?"

Just then, Nikhil's flat door creaked open, unveiling a shocking sight. Priya and her friends were all packed up, attempting to make a swift exit.

Priya, caught off guard, shared a stunned glance with her mother. Fueled by anger, Priya's mother confronted her daughter, while Priya's friends skillfully made a hasty retreat, opting for the stairs instead of the lift, leaving Priya to face the consequences.

Priya's mother turned towards Nikhil, her eyes filled with a mix of disappointment and accusation. "You knew all this, and yet you were trying to save her," she asserted.

Nikhil, overwhelmed with shame, offered a sincere apology to Priya's mother, admitting, "I just didn't want to create a scene, so I was trying to avoid telling you anything."

Priya's mother shifted her gaze to Priya, who stood there, holding plastic bags filled with trash. Snatching one of the bags from her, Priya's mother inspected its contents – empty beer bottles and pizza boxes. With a stern expression, she handed the bag back to Priya, instructing her, "After getting rid of the trash, come straight home." Without another word, Priya's mother stormed back into her house.

As Nikhil and Priya exchanged glances, Nikhil, still feeling apologetic, broke the silence. "Sorry for all the mess," he said.

Priya, curious, questioned him, "You were trying to save me?"

Nikhil met her gaze and replied, "I just didn't want your mother to get mad at you."

Taking the garbage bag, Priya mumbled, "Once I enter my home, I'll be dead anyway." Left to think about what was happening, Nikhil went into his room, wondering what would happen next.

Meanwhile, Vedant woke up from his nap. He found himself lying on the staircase of Malavika's Bungalow entrance porch. To his surprise, Malavika stood right in front of him, holding the same suitcase she had taken when she left. She looked stunned, mouth agape. Vedant quickly got up and attempted to explain.

"I was supposed to come and help you on Monday, but I completely forgot about it. I remembered at night, so I came here and found the door locked. I thought I should wait for a while and ended up falling asleep," Vedant explained.

Malavika dropped her bag and replied, "I didn't expect that you'd come and help. It's a good thing you forgot because I just arrived, and I'm sorry you had to wait for me."

Vedant seized the opportunity, saying, "Now that I'm here, I can help you unpack."

A smile spread across Malavika's face as she walked towards him, inviting him into her home.

Back at Samrat's house, Samrat found himself up early, pondering over whether to send a text message to Varsha.

His mother was having her breakfast and noticed his restlessness. She looked at Samrat and remarked, "Is something wrong? You keep checking your phone, and you never get up this early unless you have to go to work. What's going on? Is it about someone? if it is so, then why don't you just call her instead of hesitating so much?"

Surprised by his mother's keen observation, Samrat quickly asked, "How did you know?"

His mother casually replied, "Just made a wild guess."

Samrat pressed on, "How did you know it was Varsha?"

To her surprise, his mother said, "Varsha? I didn't know it was Varsha. I just thought it was some girl you liked. But what's this about Varsha? Didn't she reject you? Why are you still after her?"

Taking a moment to collect his thoughts, Samrat confessed, "It was my fault. I made her reject me. I just didn't want an arranged marriage, so I told her to reject me."

His mother, now in shock, admonished him, saying, "This is your mess to clean. Don't get me involved, and don't do anything stupid. There are plenty of other girls out there. Next time, think twice before making a hasty decision." With that, Samrat's mother picked up her empty plate and headed to the kitchen.

Samrat seethed with frustration; he grabbed his phone and impulsively messaged Varsha, 'Hi, good morning, how is it going?' and hit send. Almost immediately, a realization hit him like a ton of bricks – what a dumb move! He smacked his head in frustration, regretting the impulsive message. Determined to salvage the situation, he tried to delete the message before Varsha could read it.

In the midst of this digital crisis, a reply from Varsha popped up – a simple 'Hi.'

Samrat, now caught in the whirlwind of emotions, couldn't believe he actually got a message from her. Panic set in as he wracked his brain for the perfect response. Not wanting to waste any time, he hastily typed, 'Let's meet,' and hit send, anxiously awaiting her reply.

As minutes ticked by, there was no response from Varsha. Samrat's anxiety grew, and just when he thought it was game over, the message ringtone echoed through the room.

Varsha's reply finally arrived – 'What for?' Samrat broke into a nervous sweat; he was at a loss for words. Despite the pressure, he managed to type, 'Just a casual meet-up, can we be friends?'

The digital conversation hung in the air, but there was no reply from Varsha. Samrat, with a sinking feeling, concluded that she might not respond. The uncertainty of the situation lingered, leaving Samrat in a state of suspense and self-doubt.

Back at Malavika's place, Vedant had been lending a hand with the unpacking, pushing furniture around and setting up the new home. Sofas, tables, and a bunch of other stuff got rearranged as they worked side by side. While Vedant was busy organizing one room, Malavika took charge of the other.

Vedant couldn't help but notice she had multiple computer screens, keyboards, and not one but two CPU machines. A bit curious, he finally popped the question, "So, what do you do for a living?"

Malavika shot him a smile, "I'm a film editor. Currently, I am working on a TV serial project and I am a freelancer." She tossed the question back at him, "And you? Student or something?"

Quick on his toes, Vedant responded, "I finished my college long back, it's been years."

Malavika asked Vedant "How old are you?" Vedant hesitated then lied about his age to Malavika, he said "I am 27."

She looked at him suspiciously, but before she could dive deeper, Vedant spilled more details, "Now, I work at my dad's garage. We've got a big team. I learned everything from him, but I'm not into fixing stuff. I'm into transforming cars, you know, modifications. Let me show you some pictures?"

Vedant quickly takes his phone out and shows Malavika some of the photographs to Malavika, who was genuinely is impressed. "It's crazy how you turn these cars upside down. The before and after shots are mind-blowing. How do you even do it?" she asked.

Vedant spilled the beans, "Well, we've got engineers for the tech stuff, but I'm the bodywork guy. I chop the top of the car, sometimes the back of the car and sometimes change the door, there is a lot of cutting and fixing, but I am lucky to have great tools and a kickass team. you should come and visit my garage, it's neat and clean, pimped up garage you'll ever see."

Excitedly, Malavika agreed, "I'd love to. I love cars. Though, I'm more into classic cars."

Vedant, being the curious type, probed, "Any favorites?"

"James Bond's Aston Martin," she replied with a grin.

"The one with the ejection seat?" Vedant chuckled.

Malavika laughed, "Yes, the Aston Martin DB5."

"You've got good taste," Vedant complimented, earning another laugh.

Just as their conversation hit a high, a delivery guy knocked on the door. Lunch had arrived, and they took a break to freshen up before sharing a meal together.

And so, amidst laughter and stories, Vedant and Malavika continued to explore the unfolding chapters of their newfound friendship in that cozy, newly arranged space.

Samrat sat at the dining table, sharing an afternoon meal with his mother. A plate in one hand, his phone in the other, he skillfully juggled both, taking bites between swipes and scrolls. His mother, in between her own bites, kept a watchful eye on her son.

Unexpectedly, a message from Varsha popped up on Samrat's screen. It read, 'We can meet in the evening at a coffee shop if it's okay.' A sudden spark of joy lit up Samrat's face. With a swift reply, typed with the same hand that held the phone, he conveyed his agreement. A silly smile lingered on his lips, catching his mother's attention.

Intrigued, she stared at him, questioning the source of that sudden burst of happiness. Samrat, caught off guard, swiftly wiped the grin off his face, he pretended as if nothing extraordinary had just occurred and resumed his lunch, leaving his mother pondering over the secret smile that had momentarily danced on her son's lips.

Back at Malavika's house, after lunch, Vedant was ready to leave. Her house was almost set now. Malavika came out into the front yard to thank him for all the work he had done.

Vedant was sitting on his bike, ready to depart. Malavika stopped him and said, "Thank you for helping me out."

Vedant replied, "You have my number; call me anytime for anything, and I'll be there."

Malavika noticed Vedant's bike and asked, "Where is your helmet?"

Vedant said, "I came here in a hurry, but anyway, I don't wear a helmet because I drive this bike locally."

Hearing this, Malavika said, "Please don't ride a bike; it's not safe, and it's worse without a helmet."

Vedant was shocked to hear this. He said, "I am a safe rider, and besides, I have been riding bikes and cars since I was 15, so don't worry, I'll drive safe."

Malavika calmed herself down and said, "I guess you're right. It's just that I got worried. I usually worry when I see anyone on a bike."

Vedant asked, "Why do you worry so much?"

Malavika replied, "It's because my brother died from a bike accident, and that's why I worry. I am sure you ride well. I guess I am overreacting. Just take care of yourself."

Vedant said, "Sorry to hear about your brother." Malavika smiled and said, "It's okay."

Vedant smiled back, waved her goodbye, and drove off home.

In the evening, Samrat got ready for his date. He was dressed up well, sporting a smile that practically reached his ears. His mother couldn't help but stare at him, a mix of curiosity and concern on her face. Samrat met her gaze and said, 'I am going out on a date with Varsha.'

His mother didn't utter a word. She simply behaved as if it was just another day, casually entering the kitchen.

Samrat glanced at his watch; even though he was early, he didn't want to take any chances of being late. Determined not to keep Varsha waiting, he hopped on his bike and took off well in advance.

Upon reaching, Samrat noticed that Varsha was already waiting for him. A hint of panic struck him as he quickly checked his watch, fearing he might be running late.

He said, "I must have gotten confused about the timing, sorry for being late."

To his surprise, Varsha smiled warmly and reassured him, "Relax, you're early. I was actually out, and when I got back, I decided not to go home and change, but instead wait for you here.'

Samrat felt a wave of relief and a smile naturally formed on his face. He replied, 'So, which coffee shop do you have in mind?"

Varsha, with a sulking expression, suggested, "Let's not go to a coffee shop; I am hungry. I think I'll have an early dinner."

Samrat nodded and said, "Very well, there's a restaurant nearby; let's go there."

But Varsha wanted to go somewhere else, she said, "I know a place; let's go there instead. It's a small joint, it will be quiet now with fewer customers, it gets busy later on and it's open till late in the night."

Excited about the prospect of discovering a new place, Samrat exclaimed, "I love finding new restaurants, especially hidden ones. Let's go then."

Varsha added, "Leave your bike here; it's not far from here, and I am in no mood to spoil my hair. So, let's walk." Samrat grinned and replied, "Lead on."

After strolling for a while on the main road, Varsha abruptly took a quick turn. A staircase led downwards, and right next to it was a beautiful small restaurant that caught Samrat's eye. It reminded him of those charming little eateries in Italy, radiating a similar cozy ambiance. The restaurant featured a brick wall texture, old-school windows, a vertical signboard, a white canopy attached outside, and several small tables and chairs beneath it. Beautiful lights and numerous flower pots adorned the place.

Varsha noticed Samrat's admiration and smiled. "I knew you would love this place. Let's go inside," she suggested.

Samrat, intrigued, asked, "Why not outside?"

Varsha explained, "I have been here before, and I have my favorite spot inside next to the window."

They entered and occupied Varsha's preferred spot – a small table with chairs opposite each other. The table was draped in an old-school white tablecloth with red check-pattern lines. Varsha and Samrat sat facing each other, exchanging smiles. Both seemed to be at a loss for words. Meanwhile, the chef dropped by and greeted them.

Samrat asked for the menu, but Varsha replied, "There's no menu here."

She glanced at the chef and inquired, "What's today's special?"

The chef presented them with five choices. Varsha turned to Samrat and asked, "What would you like to have?"

Samrat, being easygoing, replied, "Everything sounds great; I'll have what you are having."

Varsha signaled to the chef, saying, "We will have linguine with clams and get us two ginger ales while we wait for the food."

The chef's daughter entered the restaurant, and the chef instructed her to serve the drinks before disappearing into the kitchen.

Samrat, taking in the charming atmosphere, shared, "I always dreamt of having a restaurant like this one, somewhere hidden, not out in the open. It makes the restaurant special."

As the waitress served the drinks, Varsha added, "The whole family works here. The chef has two daughters and a son; they all work here. I sometimes come here with my mom."

Samrat smiled. Varsha then shifted the conversation, asking, "How was your trip to Goa?"

Samrat replied, "It was great, I had fun." After a brief pause, he continued, "Listen, about our meeting at home, I am sorry for rejecting the idea of an arranged marriage, and also for making you reject me. I should not have done that."

Varsha, understandingly, said, "It's okay. I guess I am moving on."

Samrat turned to Varsha and asked, "Are you serious about this Vinod guy?"

The delectable aroma of the just-arrived food filled the air, inviting them to indulge. Without wasting any time, they eagerly started to eat. As they savored the delicious meal, the conversation shifted, and Samrat inquired, "What do you do for a living?"

Varsha responded, "I'll tell you if you promise not to tell anyone."

Samrat, with a playful smirk, teased, "Are you a spy?"

Varsha giggled at the playful banter. However, a small piece of pasta dropped onto her dress unnoticed. Samrat, in an attempt to be helpful, pulled out a tissue paper and tried to remove the pasta from her chest. Unexpectedly, his gesture caught Varsha off guard, and her jaws dropped as it felt like he was pinching her breast.

In a swift reflex, Varsha snatched the tissue paper from Samrat's hand, making him realize his unintended mistake. He stammered, "I am sorry," feeling ashamed as he sat quietly, focusing on his food.

Varsha, attempting to rub off the sauce mark from her dress with the same tissue, glanced at Samrat. In the midst of her efforts, she found the situation amusing and smiled. Samrat, still feeling embarrassed, continued eating, avoiding eye contact.

Varsha, tossing the tissue aside, smiled and said, "You can relax. How's the food?" This brought a smile to Samrat's face, and he nodded, gesturing that the food was indeed good.

After the meal, Varsha suggested, "I have to show you one more place."

Samrat replied, "Lead on." Varsha guided him to another lane, where in the corner stood a brightly lit ice cream truck. It wasn't the glamorous Hollywood version Ice cream truck, but a desi rendition.

Varsha said, "He makes amazing Faloodas. What flavor would you like?" Samrat looked at Varsha and said, "I'll have what you are having."

Varsha called for two Rose-flavored Faloodas, reigniting their conversation. "So, you didn't tell me what you do for a living?"

While handing Samrat one of the disposable glasses, Varsha replied, "It's controversial."

Samrat widened his eyes and asked, "What do you mean by that?"

Varsha explained, "I am an artist. I paint, I draw and I make comic strips. I am also a writer, so right now, I am a graphic artist and writer who creates Japanese-style comics."

Samrat, intrigued, inquired, "This sounds amazing. What is so controversial about it?"

Varsha looked into Samrat's eyes and said, "I am an Erotic graphic novel artist, and I work for a Japanese Adult Manga."

Samrat was surprised, initially silent, and then he asked, "So you do your work here and then what? mail it to Japan?"

Varsha confirmed, "Yes, also I have been to Japan a couple of times, but my parents think it was for some training purpose my company sent me."

Samrat asked, "So nobody in your family knows?"

Varsha admitted, "I just didn't know how to tell them about this."

Samrat then questioned, "And Vinod?"

Varsha replied, "He doesn't have to know all this because I decided long back, after marriage, I am going to quit everything."

Samrat observed the sadness on her face as she shared this. He, too, felt a sense of sadness, understanding that she had revealed everything because she wasn't marrying him.

Trying to gauge the situation, Samrat asked, "So have you decided to marry Vinod?"

Varsha looked at Samrat and said, "It's an arranged marriage thing. Let's see where it goes."

Samrat walked Varsha home, and upon reaching there, he expressed, "Thank you for giving me a chance and not ignoring me. It was wonderful spending this evening with you."

Varsha smiled and replied, "Ditto." Samrat picked up his parked bike and left.

THREE

TODAY IS THE MONDAYEST WEDNESDAY EVER.

Wednesday arrived, and the gang was meant to be back at work on Monday. But, the weekend holiday stretched from Thursday to Tuesday. People gripe about Mondays being the worst for work, but this Wednesday felt heavier, making the return more difficult than ever.

Samrat found himself back in his kitchen domain. Most jobs are either a test of physical endurance or a mental challenge, but kitchens demand both.

In a thriving restaurant, the team is divided into three groups: the delightful front-end crew, the shrewd managers, and a miscellaneous crew of underpaid misfits responsible for cooking your food.

Unless you've worked in a bustling kitchen, it's tough to fathom the chaotic ballet of a kitchen rush. Coded language filled the air as orders echoed through the bustling space. Multiple chefs run around to and fro in that compact area – some are using hot pans, another one running with a knife, and some yelling while balancing a pot of steaming stock. Amidst this organized chaos, some chefs were engrossed in station clean-ups, others wrestled with dishes, and a dedicated workstation became the epicenter for prepping, cooking, and plating. Within the culinary storm, waiters anxiously waited for the ready food plates.

They get a 5 minute' smoke break, few chefs along with Samrat hang out at the back of the kitchen, some of them smoke, some of them have a drink and some like Samrat take a quick bite. Five minutes was not over yet, an invisible kitchen conductor signaled them back. With a collective sigh, the chefs abandoned their momentary break, hurrying back to their stations, ready to resume the symphony of sizzling pans and clattering plates.

Nikhil found himself in his boss's cabin, facing a storm of lectures for taking extra leaves. The boss, in a fit of anger, went on about Nikhil's irresponsibility and alleged laziness at work. Throughout the lecture, Nikhil remained silent, absorbing the words like a sponge. Finally, he apologized and left the cabin, nursing a growing headache.

Retreating to his cubicle, Nikhil sat down and began typing away on his keyboard. The work itself was something he enjoyed; each new project brought fresh opportunities to learn. However, the thorn in his side was the office culture. Although the official working hours were from 9 to 6, nobody seemed to budge at 6 in the evening.

As the clock struck six, the eerie silence of a stationary workforce filled the office. Nikhil, having completed his tasks for the day, found himself twiddling his thumbs. Leaving on time wasn't an option. If he dared to make a move, he'd inevitably face raised eyebrows and comments like, "You're leaving early today?"

To make matters worse, Nikhil's manager had a knack for sly tactics. He could assign time-consuming tasks at 5.50 PM, wearing a devious smile as he asked, "You still have some time to leave, right?" The double standards continued; if Nikhil arrived five minutes early, the manager would demand, "You're late. Come at least 15 minutes earlier to settle down." Yet, if Nikhil was five minutes late, all he'd hear was, "You're always late to work."

This was just one of the challenges Nikhil faces daily in his office. Office politics lurked around every corner, making his professional life as wild as a rollercoaster ride. As he navigated through the complexities of his job, he found himself juggling not only projects but also the tricky dynamics of office politics.

At the garage, Vedant's father dropped a bombshell, informing him of the mountain of pending work that needed his attention. While the freedom of working in their own garage brought a sense of liberation, the responsibilities weighed heavy on Vedant and his father. Managing a qualified team came with countless duties – ensuring salaries were met, basic needs were fulfilled, safety protocols were in place, and a favorable working environment was maintained. On top of it all, customer service required meticulous handling to guarantee repeat business.

Running a business, Vedant realized, was a unique venture. It wasn't just about earning for one's family; but also for an extended family at work. Vedant's passion for modifying cars had created a niche customer base. However, not every project was a success. Some ventures failed, and at times, clients backed out, leaving Vedant in a quandary with a half-finished vehicle.

Eager to embark on a new project, Vedant shared his plan with his father. He had set his sights on an old Fiat Padmini classic taxi that he intended to transform. Vedant's father, a voice of reason, cautioned, " You better do a custom job if you have a customer ready to pay for it, or it's just a waste of money."

Unfazed, Vedant revealed, "This time, it's different. I'm working on it as a gift for a friend."

His father arched an eyebrow, offering a piece of advice, "Just be certain she's 'the one,' or you might end up gifting her something quite expensive."

Vedant was surprised his Dad figured out it was for a girl, nevertheless, he went back to working on the car.

Later that evening, Nikhil boarded a bus headed home, scooter keys still in the possession of Priya. Seated next to the window, his thoughts drifted towards Priya. Pulling out his phone, he decided to check her social media account.

Priya's profile showcased a series of videos. It seemed like a weekly ritual for her, with a ten-minute video providing a deeper dive into her life, complemented by daily one-minute snippets.

Nikhil scrolled through the collection and clicked on the latest 10-minute video.

Opening the video, Priya greeted her audience, "Hi friends, let's see what's cooking in my life in this week's video."

The narration unfolded as she shared snippets of her day. She began by revealing that she had skipped breakfast due to the rush to college. Despite being almost late, she managed to catch up on the first-hour lecture.

The day unfolded with back-to-back classes, leaving Priya with no time for a break. Hunger gnawed at her, and it wasn't until the third lecture that she made her way to the canteen.

However, an unexpected sight awaited her – A friend next to her tapped on her shoulder and showed her to the food counter below, there were many chip packets and biscuit pouches stacked on the glass counter below and a small Mouse was struggling between the packages and was trying to get to the other end, she called the canteen guy and said: "There is a mouse in your counter." And she returns the food tray. The canteen guy said, "It's not refundable." Undeterred, Priya quipped, "Feed it to the mouse; you're a rat-infested canteen."

Enduring the final lecture on an empty stomach, Priya and her friends later sought refuge in a nearby restaurant, indulging in a much-needed feast. The video captured her day in vivid detail, from studies at home to helping her mother cook, and finally, spending quality time with friends in the evening.

Priya concluded with a cheerful sign-off, "So, friends, this was it for today. Let's see what's cooking in my life next week. Till then, enjoy my short videos." The bus rumbled on, but Nikhil couldn't shake off the smile that Priya's day had brought to his face.

Intrigued, Nikhil scrolled down to check Priya's short videos. The clip began with Priya rising from her bed, gazing into the mirror, and chirping, "Hi friends, let's see what's cooking in my life today."

The scenes unfolded seamlessly - brushing her teeth, getting dressed, picking up her bag, and leaving the house. The next snippet captured her boarding a bus, then squeezing into a crowded one, humorously remarking, "This is the life of a student."

The narrative continued as she entered her class, giving viewers a glimpse into the routine of a student's day. The final scene depicted Priya with her friends, chilling out and bidding everyone a cheerful goodbye. The simplicity of her daily life painted a relatable picture for Nikhil.

As the bus trundled through the city, Nikhil couldn't help but appreciate the ordinary yet genuine moments Priya shared with her online audience. It was a brief escape into someone else's routine, a refreshing change from the complexities of his own life.

A smile played on Nikhil's lips, and he couldn't resist the temptation to see the next video. Scrolling down, he found a clip that caught his attention. This one was all about his beloved scooter, the Lambretta.

In the video, Priya and her friends embarked on a ride, joining other girls cruising on motorcycles. They traversed through the city and eventually halted at a picturesque riverside. The group immersed themselves in the beauty of the surroundings, capturing the moments with countless pictures.

Nikhil watched in surprise as Priya skillfully handled the scooter, showcasing a side of her he hadn't seen before. The joy on her face and the company with her friends made the video a delightful watch. But what warmed Nikhil's heart the most was seeing his cherished scooter, the Lambretta, taking the spotlight in the video.

The simple joy of watching Priya and his scooter on an adventure brought a sense of happiness to Nikhil, momentarily easing the strains of the day. The videos offered a unique window into Priya's world, and unwittingly, she became a source of solace for Nikhil, even if just through the lens of a smartphone screen.

Nikhil found himself captivated by several of Priya's uploaded videos, losing track of time. Unaware that his stop had arrived, he disembarked from the bus, still engrossed in Priya's short clips. Lost in the digital world, he strolled towards his building, suddenly remembering he needed to buy some essentials.

Entering the local corner store, Nikhil continued watching Priya's videos while picking up his Kirana needs. The shopkeeper handed him the bag, and as Nikhil pocketed the change, he happened to glance up and saw Priya standing right in front of him.

Caught off guard, she queried, "What's so funny? What are you watching?" Panic set in for Nikhil. Swiftly turning off his phone, he discreetly stowed it away.

Meanwhile, the shopkeeper handed Priya a bag, mentioning he had recorded the items on her tab. Nikhil lingered, and when Priya asked if he was waiting for someone, he stammered, "No."

She gestured for him to lead the way, and they walked in silence for a while.

Breaking the quiet, Priya remarked, "I saw you getting off the bus," and handed over the scooter keys. "Sorry, I forgot to give it back. Thank you for trusting me with it."

Nikhil, still processing the unexpected encounter, managed a nod and a faint smile. The exchange left an air of curiosity hanging between them, a connection sparked by a chance meeting at the local corner store.

Nikhil was happy to get his scooter key back. As they walked together, Priya broke the silence, "I need your help with a college project."

"What's it about?" Nikhil asked.

"I have to make a documentary movie, but I'm clueless about the topic. And, to top it off, I don't have a budget. So, for starters, I'm just gathering a crew who would work for free," Priya explained.

Nikhil raised an eyebrow, "So you're recruiting me as one of your crew?"

Priya burst into laughter before replying, "Yes, will you help me?"

Nikhil smiled, "Okay, I'll do my best."

"Thank you. I want to be a film director someday," Priya confessed.

"Wow, I'm sure you'll do well," Nikhil replied.

Upon reaching their floor, Priya's mother stood at the door, her expression stern as she stared at Nikhil. This made Nikhil nervous, and he managed to give Priya's mother a hesitant smile. However, she didn't reciprocate, just maintaining a cold look.

Unaware of the tension, Priya bid Nikhil goodbye, "See you tomorrow!" and entered her house. Nikhil struggled with his keys, eventually unlocking the door. He glanced back at Priya's mom and offered another smile, but she ignored it and entered her house, leaving Nikhil to ponder, "How am I going to deal with all this?"

Little did Nikhil know, that this encounter with Priya's mother was just the beginning of a new set of challenges that awaited him in the days to come.

After a tiring day in the kitchen, Samrat left for home. He walked out to the staff parking area, started his bike, and headed towards the main road, where the restaurant's entrance was visible.

While making a turn, he spotted Varsha and Vinod, dressed for the occasion and seemingly happy in each other's company. Varsha, engrossed in conversation with Vinod, didn't notice Samrat.

Vinod eventually left, leaving Samrat contemplating whether to approach Varsha. Just as he was deciding, Vinod's car pulled in. Varsha got in, and the car drove off. Samrat, caught in the moment, decided to follow them. The car stopped at Varsha's place, and she exited. After a brief chat by the car window, she bid farewell, and the car sped away. Samrat quickly parked his bike near Varsha.

Just as Varsha was about to enter her gate, she turned and saw Samrat. He greeted her with a simple "Hi."

Varsha, looking suspicious, questioned, "Were you following us?"

Samrat denied it, saying, "I just came back from work." Trying to ease the tension, Varsha asked, "Where do you work?"

Samrat replied, "I work at O MY." Playfully, he inquired, "Have you been to that restaurant?"

Varsha admitted, "I was just there with Vinod."

Samrat explained, "We must have left at the same time, and that's why you thought I was following you. By the way, how did you like the food there?"

Varsha praised, "It was good, I love it."

Samrat probed, "So, have things fixed yet?"

Varsha responded, "Not yet, let's see where it goes."

A strange silence lingered before Varsha stated, "I've got to go, it's getting late."

Samrat concurred, "Oh yeah, it is late. See you then."

Varsha entered her building gate, and Samrat waited, watching her until she was safely inside before leaving himself. The night held unanswered questions and a sense of uncertainty for Samrat.

Later that night, Samrat took a bold step and sent a text message to Varsha, "You were looking good in that dress," accompanied by a smiley face. However, Varsha did not reply. Samrat anxiously waited for a long time before eventually falling asleep.

The next morning, as Samrat woke up and checked his phone, he found a notification of a message from Varsha. Excitedly, he opened the message to find a simple 'Thank you.' The timestamp revealed that Varsha had replied at 3:15 in the night. Samrat, feeling a connection, responded with a 'Good morning' message, adding a heart icon. He then went about his daily routine.

A couple of hours later, just before leaving for work, Samrat picked up his phone, hoping to find a response. To his disappointment, there wasn't any message. He pondered whether the heart icon in his morning message was perhaps too much, leaving him with a sense of uncertainty about where things stood between him and Varsha.

Vedant decided to pay Malavika a visit, keeping in mind her dislike of motorbikes. Opting for a car, he drove to her house. Upon arrival, Vedant observed a guest chatting with Malavika on the porch. Seated in his car, Vedant could see the lively exchange between the two.

When Malavika noticed Vedant entering, she warmly introduced the guest, "This is Rukmini, my bestie. She's come all the way from Kerala to visit me." Vedant couldn't help but notice the vintage camera in Rukmini's hands.

"That's an old-looking camera," Vedant remarked.

Malavika shared, "She is a professional photographer and she takes it everywhere, she loves this old vintage roll camera because she won't know how the image turns out until she develops them – she loves the surprise."

Malavika announced that Rukmini would be staying for a week and suggested, "Why don't you show her around?" Vedant agreed.

Teasingly, Malavika commented, "You both look cute together," eliciting a synchronized protest from Rukmini and Vedant, "No way!" This amused Malavika, who burst into laughter.

Vedant, curious to know more about Rukmini, asked, "That's all you got about her?"

Malavika assured him, "Don't worry; you'll get to know more about her when you show her around."

Rukmini, inquisitive about Vedant, prompted, "You just gave him my introduction, what about his?" Rukmini asked Malavika.

Malavika, with a mischievous smile, replied, "Do you know how we met?"

Rukmini, brimming with excitement, urged, "How? Tell me everything."

Vedant, feeling a bit embarrassed, interjected, "You don't have to tell her everything." Despite Vedant's protest, Malavika proceeded to share their story, and Rukmini couldn't contain her excitement. Sensing a hint of love in the air, she playfully tried to embarrass Vedant.

Impressed with Vedant's profession, Rukmini expressed admiration for what he does for a living. Vedant, seizing the opportunity, invited her, "I'll take you to my garage and show you how I work on my cars. Plus, you can take pictures as well."

This reminder sparked Rukmini's enthusiasm, and she began capturing moments, taking many pictures of Malavika and the duo together. Vedant reciprocated by taking pictures of both Rukmini and Malavika.

The trio had a great time at Malavika's house. After lunch, Vedant suggested, "Why don't you both come to my garage? We'll have fun there."

However, Malavika, realizing her impending deadline, said, "I have work to finish today, or I won't make the deadline. Why don't you take Rukmini to your garage now? Meanwhile, I'll complete my pending work."

Finally, Vedant took Rukmini in his car, and they drove off to explore Vedant's garage.

After reaching Vedant's garage, Vedant gave Rukmini a tour, proudly showcasing his workspace. Rukmini, armed with her camera, took pictures of the fascinating machinery and tools around her.

Vedant pointed at the car he was currently working on, saying, "This is an old classic car. You must have seen our old taxis."

Rukmini nodded in agreement and asked, "So, what are your plans for this car?"

Vedant explained, "Well, I'm trying to make it look like an Aston Martin DB5. It won't be entirely accurate, but it'll be close enough. The features and the tail light match; I just have to extend the front end and chop half of the top off." Vedant continued with more technical details that went over Rukmini's head, but she politely listened, captivated by his passion.

Eventually, when Vedant paused, Rukmini brought up a personal note, "One of Malavika's favorite cars is this Aston Martin you referred to. Are you aware of that?" Vedant, perhaps intentionally, pretended not to hear and smoothly diverted the conversation, saying, "Let's go have coffee. There's a newly opened café shop around the corner."

Rukmini smiled, and the two of them headed to the café, leaving behind the world of engines and tools for a moment of relaxation and conversation.

At the coffee shop, Vedant ordered two cold coffees for them. Rukmini, sipping her coffee, dove straight into the matter, saying, "I can see that you like Malavika, but you look young. How old are you? And don't lie to me like you did to Malavika."

Vedant, caught off guard, wondered how she found out. Hesitant, he replied, "I am 22."

Rukmini, with a knowing look, pointed out, "That's an eight years' difference. You do realize that Malavika is 30, right?"

Vedant's eyebrows raised in surprise, and he admitted, "We guessed it." Rukmini, intrigued, questioned, "We?"

Vedant clarified, "Me and my friends."

Rukmini, with a sense of wisdom beyond her years, warned him, "When you'll be 30, she'll be 38. Are you ready for it?"

Vedant found himself at a loss for words. Rukmini continued, "Women look more womanly in their 30s. It's the age of beauty. If you're not serious and you just want to get laid, then please back off. She is not the one for you."

Vedant, reflecting on his feelings, admitted, "I have never done it. It's not like I have an old-school mindset or think that we should do it only after we get married. I was just never in any relationship before, not in my school days or college times. Maybe you're right; I was initially attracted by her physical appearance. But then, I am just 22, and I have zero experience in love. Love comes naturally, and I found that out after getting to know her. Our friendship has grown much more, and I like her more."

Rukmini, seemingly satisfied with his honesty, advised, "If you are serious about her and you wish to marry her, only then should you be in her life. She has already faced too much."

Vedant absorbed Rukmini's words, realizing the depth of what he was getting into and the responsibility that came with it.

Vedant, sensing the weight of Malavika's past, couldn't help but ask Rukmini, "Is it because of her brother's death?"

Rukmini paused for a moment and then replied, "I am not sure if I should tell you this, but you have to promise me not to tell her anything about what I am going to tell you. I am just sharing this because I have a feeling that she is going to reject you, and will never agree to be with you. When she does that, I want you to understand what she is going through. I don't want you to hate her. I just hope you win her heart, and she accepts you and loves you like you do."

Rukmini continued, revealing the painful chapters of Malavika's life. "Malavika lived in Kerala; her parents died in a car accident when she was young. No relatives came for the funeral, and Malavika was left alone. The neighbors realized that the reason why nobody came was that they would then have to take Malavika along, and nobody in her relatives wanted to adopt a kid. The neighbors had already taken care of the funeral, but they couldn't just leave Malavika all alone. So, they decided to raise her as their own. The neighbor already had a son named Manoj, and he was of the same age. As they grew up together, they treated both of them like siblings."

The tale of Malavika's past unfolded, shedding light on the challenges she had faced and the unique bond she shared with the neighbors who became her second family. Vedant listened intently, realizing the depth of Malavika's journey and the scars she carried.

Rukmini continued, "As they grew up, they attended the same school and later the same college. Over time, feelings blossomed between Manoj and Malavika, but the constraints of being treated like siblings in their shared home prevented them from openly expressing their love. Despite this, one afternoon Manoj was all alone in Malavika's room and in the moment he kissed Malavika on her lips, even though it was just a small peck on her lips, in that moment, Malavika felt the warmth of love."

"Their bond strengthened, and they grew closer. Sharing similar tastes and hobbies, it became evident that they were deeply in love with each other. However, the societal constraints weighed on them."

"Feeling the need to address their relationship, Malavika encouraged Manoj to talk to their parents about them. Both lacked the courage to broach the subject. Soon Manoj goes into depression and his parents don't know why this is happening. In an attempt to bring a positive change to his life, they decided to send Manoj abroad for further studies, hoping a change in surroundings might help him recover."

"However, facing Malavika again proved to be too difficult for Manoj. Despite completing his studies, Manoj finds a good job abroad and he never returns. Meanwhile, back at home, Malavika took good care of her step-parents. She pursued a career in the film industry, working as an assistant director, carving her own path despite the heartache she had endured."

"As time passed, both Malavika and Manoj resisted the pressures to get married, despite their parents' persistent efforts. After many years, Manoj made a life-altering decision. He quit his job and returned home to Kerala. His parents were overjoyed to see him back, and Manoj, too, was pleased to reunite with Malavika. They began catching up, trying to make up for the lost time. Manoj, with plans to start a business in his hometown, became busy with the endeavor. Meanwhile, their love for each other continued to strengthen."

"One day, Manoj entered Malavika's room, holding a ring. He expressed his desire to marry her and vowed to tell everything to his parents. Handing the ring to Malavika, he said, "This is a promise ring. I'll make it work." Malavika, overwhelmed with happiness, accepted the ring, although nervous about how their parents would react to this news."

Rukmini paused in her storytelling, her emotions visible. Vedant could see her eyes welling up, but Rukmini composed herself, holding back the tears.

She took a sip of her coffee and continued, "Before he could break the news to his parents, Manoj met with a bike accident and died on the spot." The weight of the tragedy hung in the air, leaving both Vedant and Rukmini in somber reflection.

Vedant, overwhelmed by the heartbreaking story, could only feel a deep sense of sadness. Rukmini continued to share the tale, saying, "He was out for his new business deal and never made it back. It was devastating for the whole family. Malavika was in shock for a long time. She quit her job and stayed home."

Rukmini went on, revealing Malavika's struggles. "Malavika decided not to tell her parents about her relationship with Manoj.

She felt that they were already saddened by their son's death, and she didn't want to give them more pain. After six months, she joined the film industry again and got very busy. Almost a year later, Malavika received a call from Bollywood, and she shifted here to Mumbai."

Curious and still absorbing the emotional narrative, Vedant asked Rukmini, "How do you know all this?" Rukmini smiled and replied, "Malavika, Manoj, and I have been together since our school days. I love Malavika, and she is my best friend. But I also had a crush on Manoj, and I knew someday I would marry him. Malavika and I shared everything, and that's how I got to know her story. Malavika also knew about my crush on Manoj. I love them both." Rukmini's eyes welled up with emotion once again, revealing the depth of her connection with her friends and the shared pain they had endured.

Rukmini remarked, "It's been long; Malavika will be worried."

Vedant assured, "Don't worry; I'll drop you in a jiffy." He takes his bike out and takes Rukmini back to Malavika's place, on reaching there, he drops her a little further from the gates.

"You better walk from here; Malavika doesn't like me riding bikes without a helmet," Vedant advised.

Rukmini teased, "Oh, looks like she has some feelings for you."

Curious, Vedant asked, "Do you think I have a chance with her?"

Rukmini smiled and nodded at him. She then added, "I'll be leaving in a couple of days. Before I go, please come and meet me once again."

With that, she walked towards the gate. Vedant waited until she got inside. Emotionally stirred by the conversation, Vedant decided to clear his head by taking a long ride on his bike.

FOUR

HOW HARD CAN IT BE?

Nikhil, a 31-year-old software engineer, found himself entangled in an unexpected love story with Priya, a vivacious 19-year-old college student. As they navigated the complexities of their relationship, they stumbled upon a unique challenge.

How Hard can it be?

The doorbell rang, startling Nikhil out of his thoughts. He opened the door to find Priya standing there, her infectious smile lighting up his world. Before he could utter a word, she breezed past him and into his home.

Nikhil's heart raced as he glanced nervously towards the door, half-expecting Priya's mother to be hovering nearby. Priya seemed to read his mind, reassuring him with a simple, "Don't worry, Mom's at the market."

Surprised by her intuition, Nikhil couldn't help but wonder how she knew.

Priya said, "Remember I told you about my college movie project?"

Nikhil nodded, his curiosity piqued. "Yes," he replied.

Seizing the opportunity, Priya launched into an animated explanation of her project, detailing its significance in her academic journey and the fierce competition among her peers. Nikhil listened intently, his admiration for Priya growing with each word she spoke.

When she finally paused for breath,

Nikhil suggested, "Why don't you sit down? I was just cooking. Let me finish up, and then we can brainstorm together."

As Priya settled onto the couch, Nikhil busied himself in the kitchen, stealing glances at her whenever he could. Once the meal was prepared, they sat down together, their conversation flowing effortlessly.

"Do you know what others are doing for their projects?" Nikhil inquired, genuinely interested.

Priya nodded, her expression thoughtful. "Yes, most of them are working on documentary films. Some are exploring politics, while others delve into travel and food. There are even those tackling bold topics like sex and relationships, and LGBTQ issues."

A hint of frustration crept into her voice as she added, "And then there's me, running around in circles with no clear direction."

Nikhil reached out, squeezing her hand in reassurance. "Don't worry, Priya. We'll figure it out together." Saying this he enters the kitchen.

Nikhil emerged from the kitchen, balancing two plates of food with practiced ease. "Here, try my cooking and tell me how it is," he said, a hint of nervousness in his voice.

Priya's eyes lit up as she accepted the plate, settling down at the table with Nikhil. As they ate, Nikhil couldn't contain his excitement any longer.

"I have a plan," he announced, his eyes sparkling with enthusiasm. "My friend Vedant is a car enthusiast. He's currently working on a project, but he's already halfway through. What we need is a project that's just starting out, something we can document from the very beginning."

Priya's face lit up with understanding. "That's a brilliant idea!" she exclaimed. "Please talk to Vedant and let me know. It could be the perfect opportunity for my documentary."

Nikhil finished his meal and glanced at Priya's plate, noticing that she had already polished off her food. Before he could say anything, Priya whisked the plates away to the kitchen sink.

"You don't have to do this," Nikhil protested, but Priya waved him off with a smile.

"It's okay," she replied. "This is what I'm good at. I may not know how to cook – thank goodness for your culinary skills – but I can handle the dishes. I've always joked that if I ever get married, my future husband better knows how to cook because I certainly can't!"

Feeling a bit awkward, Nikhil cleared his throat. "I think I should call Vedant and check if he can help," he said, excusing himself.

Exiting the kitchen, Nikhil dialed Vedant's number. Vedant answered promptly, and Nikhil wasted no time in explaining the situation.

After listening intently, Vedant suggested, "I'm planning to watch a movie with Malavika and her friend Rukmini. Why don't you bring Priya along? That way, I get to meet her, and we can discuss her college project."

Nikhil hesitated. "I'll have to ask her; her mother is kind of a strict person."

"Okay, ask her and then call me back," Vedant replied before ending the call.

Nikhil said, "Wait hold on she's here at my place, let me ask her now."

Vedant was surprised and said "She's at your place? what kind of strict mother does she have?" Vedant teased.

Nikhil unintentionally blurted out "Her mother is not at home." causing him to cringe inwardly, he shouldn't have given that information knowing that Vedant would surely pull his leg.

Vedant sarcastically said, "Bravo my friend, now will you please hurry and ask her?"

Brushing off the comment, Nikhil asked Priya, "Would you like to go watch a movie? Vedant has asked us if we can join him and his two lady friends."

Priya agreed, and Nikhil informed Vedant of their decision. "The show is at 6 in the evening. Be there an hour early so we can discuss," Vedant instructed.

"We'll be there at 5. See you then," Nikhil confirmed, feeling a surge of excitement.

Priya smiled gratefully. "Thank you for helping. At 4:30, I'll be waiting next to your scooter."

Later, at 4:30, when Nikhil headed to his parking spot, he spotted Priya. She was donning a lovely yellow pop Schiffli knee-length dress, with a hint of makeup enhancing her features. "So, ready for our movie date?" she asked with a grin.

Nikhil smiled, he composed himself and made his way to his scooter. Starting it up, he gestured for her to hop on. However, he noticed a change in Priya's demeanor; her expression turned serious.

Realizing that he should have said something, Nikhil glanced back at her as they rode away from the building. "You're looking beautiful in that dress," he complimented, hoping to lift her spirits.

Priya couldn't help but smile at his words. As they zoomed off, Priya's mother caught sight of them from the top of the building. She stood in the open corridor, watching them together, her worries starting to brew.

As Priya and Nikhil strolled into the mall, they found themselves drawn to the bustling food court. "Why don't we buy the tickets? What if the shows are full?" Priya inquired, a hint of concern in her voice.

Nikhil flashed a reassuring grin. "Vedant has already got our tickets, so no worries," he replied.

A smile instantly lit up Priya's face at the news. Spotting a trio approaching from a distance, she eagerly grabbed Nikhil's hand and subtly gestured towards them with her eyes.

Nikhil turned to see who she was indicating. "Yeah, it's them. How did you guess?" he asked, intrigued.

Priya chuckled softly. "Two girls, one boy," she explained.

When Vedant, Malavika, and Rukmini finally joined Nikhil and Priya, there was an unexpected moment of recognition between Vedant and Priya. "You?" Vedant exclaimed, pointing at her in disbelief.

Priya glanced at Vedant, then back at Nikhil. "This is your friend," she stated matter-of-factly.

Vedant's eyes widened in surprise. "You're dating this college kid?" he asked Nikhil incredulously.

"I am in college, but I am not a kid. I am in my second year," Priya clarified, her tone firm.

Rukmini, observing the interaction between Vedant and Priya, couldn't help but comment, "Wow, these two kids look cute together."

"We are not kids," Vedant and Priya protested simultaneously, their voices blending into a chorus of denial.

Nikhil intervened with a chuckle. "Then behave like one. Let's start with Vedant. How do you know Priya?" he prompted.

Vedant composed himself before replying, "I was in my 2nd year, and she was in 11th. We went to the same college."

Malavika, intrigued by the conversation, began to calculate. "You're 22?" she asked Vedant, her eyes widening in surprise.

Vedant nodded sheepishly. "Yes," he admitted.

Rukmini joined in the questioning, curious about their connection. "But how did you guys know each other? You were not from the same class," she pointed out.

Priya eagerly jumped in to explain. "He and his gang used to hang out on our junior college campus, to check out girls," she revealed.

Vedant quickly added, "We were there to help you with our old notes, and you took my notes and never returned them."

Nikhil interjected, sensing the conversation veering off track. "Okay, we get it; you both were college buddies. Now let's get down to business and discuss her college project," he suggested.

Malavika, glancing at her watch, proposed a change of plans. "I think we should do this after the movie; it's almost showtime now," she suggested.

Agreeing with Malavika, they decided to prioritize entertainment and headed off to catch the movie first.

The movie turned out to be surprisingly long, and as they emerged from the theater, the gang found themselves in high spirits. The aroma of food wafting from the nearby food court tempted them, and they decided to prolong their time together with a dinner there.

But Priya hesitated, mindful of the time. "It's late, and mom will be worried," she voiced her concern.

Vedant, ever the practical one, chimed in. "I know the real purpose for you to come was for your college project. When do you have to submit this project?" he inquired.

"We have two months to complete it," Priya revealed.

Vedant suggested an alternative plan. "Why don't you guys come to my garage then? We can discuss, and you'll also get some ideas for your documentary when you see my work and my garage," he proposed.

Priya and Nikhil exchanged glances, considering Vedant's offer. Finally, they both nodded in agreement. "That sounds like a great idea," Priya replied.

With Vedant's proposition settled, they bid farewell to the food court and set off home.

Priya mustered up the courage to ask Nikhil if she could drive the scooter. With a gentle smile, Nikhil agreed, and they set off towards home, the wind whipping through their hair as they navigated the streets. Finally, they reached the parking lot, and as they dismounted the scooter, Priya turned to Nikhil with a question burning in her mind.

"Tell me something, were you jealous when you found out Vedant and I were friends in college?" she queried, her voice tinged with curiosity.

Nikhil was caught off guard by her directness. He attempted to brush off the question casually. "No... in college, you're bound to have boyfriends, it's no big deal," he replied coolly.

However, Priya could sense a hint of jealousy in Nikhil's tone. Playing along, she decided to share a bit of her own history. "That's good to know. Even though I am single now, I had two boyfriends before. One lasted a year when I was in 12th, and the other lasted for six months when I was in my first year. But Vedant and I never dated; we just pissed each other off," she revealed with a chuckle.

Nikhil acknowledged her words with a simple "I see." As they waited for the lift to arrive, there was a brief pause in the conversation.

Suddenly, Nikhil spoke up. "Aren't you going to ask me about my girlfriends?" he inquired, a hint of playfulness in his voice.

Priya flashed him a smile. "Well, I don't care," she responded teasingly. "I just live in the present."

The lift door opened, and they entered, standing facing the door as it ascended. When they reached their respective floors, Priya's mother was waiting outside. Her stern expression immediately put Nikhil on edge.

Without a word, Priya hurried inside, leaving Nikhil to face her mother alone. Priya's mother follows her in and slams the door behind her.

Nikhil knew this wasn't a great timing, he was a little worried and instead of entering his house, he stood outside in the open corridor staring into the distance as he pondered the unexpected turn of events.

The next day found Nikhil at home, having taken a rare day off from work. He had slept in late and skipped breakfast, and by the time he rose from bed, it was already noon. Feeling the pangs of hunger, he decided to prepare lunch after a quick shower.

Just as he was getting ready to cook, the doorbell rang, breaking the silence of his apartment.

Surprised, Nikhil went to answer it, and to his astonishment, he found Priya's mom standing on the doorstep. She was dressed in a striking black bodycon dress, her hair cascading down in loose waves, and her makeup adding an air of sophistication to her appearance.

"Can I come in?" she asked, her voice calm and composed.

"Yes, ma'am," Nikhil replied automatically, taken aback by her unexpected visit.

"Call me Reena," she insisted with a smile.

"Reena?" Nikhil repeated, slightly perplexed.

"Yes, do I look like ma'am types to you?" Priya's mother teased, her tone playful.

"No, you look beautiful and very young, I must say," Nikhil complimented sincerely.

Priya's mother chuckled softly. "I had Priya when I was 22, so you see I am not as old as you thought I was."

"No, I never thought of you as old," Nikhil assured her. "In fact, Priya's good looks do come from you; I can see the resemblance."

Priya's mother gracefully took a seat, motioning for Nikhil to do the same. As he sat down, he couldn't help but feel a sense of unease. What was the purpose of her visit?

Priya's mother crossed her legs, her actions exuding confidence revealing her smooth waxed legs. Nikhil felt a flutter of discomfort in his stomach, he asked her 'What would you like coffee or tea?'

Priya's Mother gets up and sits next to Nikhil, she leans closer to him and speaks softly.

"Listen, I know you're wondering how can I have an affair with Priya's mom and what will happen when she finds out?" Priya's Mother stated matter-of-factly.

Nikhil's eyes widened in shock. "Affair?" he repeated, his voice betraying his confusion.

"Yes," Priya's Mother affirmed. "Tell me, what's wrong with me? I am a single mom; I look sexy; we both are mature. What more do you want?"

Nikhil was speechless, his mind reeling with disbelief. Priya's Mother continued her words hanging heavy in the air.

"Priya doesn't have to know about this. It's not like I am asking you to get married to me. Let's just keep this casual. We can enjoy together, but let's keep Priya out of this. If we are having this relationship, then you have to stop talking to Priya," she proposed.

Nikhil rose abruptly from his chair, his mind racing. "Don't get me wrong," he began, his voice trembling with emotion.

"You're very beautiful and sexy, any guy would love to be with you. And I am sure someday you'll find the right guy. But right now, I am not that guy."

He took a deep breath, his resolve firm. "I know you think because of my age I must have done it several times and I am looking forward to doing the same with Priya, but that is not the case. I think I am old-school in this department, I have never done it before, and I would love to get intimate with someone I love or someone whom I'll marry. The casual thing doesn't work for me."

With that, Nikhil stood his ground, his heart heavy with the weight of the conversation.

Priya's mom's expression shifted, her behavior becoming more serious as the previous air of seduction dissipated. She regarded Nikhil with a somber gaze before speaking.

"You're a good guy," she began, her voice carrying a tone of sincerity. "When Priya was young, her father left us for another woman. He didn't even divorce me; he just left. When Priya grew up, I told her everything. She grew up without her father, and that's why I think she's unable to handle relationships. She had many boyfriends, but she ended up breaking up with them."

Her eyes clouded with emotion as she continued, "I have read somewhere that girls without fathers end up with an older guy, and then you came along. I just want her to marry someone close to her age. That's all I am asking."

Nikhil responded thoughtfully, "First of all, I am not old; I am just older than Priya. You have to understand that in today's society, many people have been taught to think and behave in certain ways. Some folks tend to blame women a lot because they feel insecure themselves. They believe in lots of untrue ideas that are spread widely in mainstream culture. For instance, they might use hurtful words like 'sluts' or 'whores' to describe sexually confident women. But there's nothing wrong with being confident in your sexuality. Also, why do we say that girls with daddy issues seek out older guys, it's been happening for centuries that some women are attracted to older men."

Priya's mom listened silently, absorbing Nikhil's perspective. After a moment of reflection, she spoke up, "You're right. I won't interfere in her love life again and I don't mind if she marries an older guy, but not right now, not at this age. Maybe she can make that decision when she grows up a little. So I request you to please stay away from her."

Nikhil nodded in understanding, though he couldn't shake off the disappointment and sadness that lingered within him. As Priya's mother left his place, he couldn't help but feel that he failed to make it work, maybe this relationship with Priya is too good to be true.

Nikhil began to distance himself from Priya, no longer willing to offer his assistance with her college project. When Priya visited him, hoping for his support, he handed her Vedant's phone number and informed her that he wouldn't be able to help her anymore.

Initially, Priya was puzzled by Nikhil's sudden change in behavior, but eventually, she realized that her mother had intervened, causing Nikhil to avoid her. This realization left Priya feeling deeply saddened and withdrawn. She became quiet and despondent, rarely speaking or using her phone. Her sadness was palpable, casting a shadow over her usual lively demeanor.

Observing her daughter's depressed state, Priya's mother couldn't help but feel a sense of guilt and remorse for unintentionally causing her distress. She wished she could undo the pain she had unknowingly imposed upon Priya, but now, all she could do was watch helplessly as her daughter struggled to cope with the fallout of their recent interactions.

A couple of days later, as Priya rushed towards the elevator door, she found Nikhil already inside. Their eyes met briefly before Priya's foot inadvertently blocked the door as she enters in and turns around and face the door, the lift door closes, they don't speak to each other, they stood in silence, facing to the door as the elevator descended.

Suddenly, the elevator came to a halt, plunging the space into darkness save for the faint glow of the emergency light. Feeling a bit nervous, Priya glanced back at Nikhil, who reassured her, "Don't worry, it takes a few minutes to go on backup battery."

Priya turned back to face the door, waiting in silence. After a moment, she spoke up, breaking the tense atmosphere. "I know my mother told you to stay away from me," she confessed.

Nikhil remained silent, prompting Priya to continue. "I guess you're not my type," she remarked quietly.

"Not your type?" Nikhil echoed, his voice tinged with curiosity.

"Yes, not my type," Priya affirmed. "I don't care who I am friends with—old, young, ugly, or beautiful. Rich or poor. All I want is that my friend should stand by me. And if I prefer someone as a boyfriend, then I want a guy who fights for his girl, not leave her. And so, you're not my type."

As if in agreement with her words, the lift light changed, and the elevator resumed its descent. "See, even the lift agrees," Priya remarked with a wry smile.

The elevator door opened, and Priya stepped out, leaving Nikhil inside. He remained there, deep in thought, pondering the weight of Priya's words. As the door closed on him, he couldn't shake the feeling that he had lost something valuable in that fleeting moment of truth.

Vedant, at 22 years old, found himself in love with an older girl, Malavika, who is 30. However, their romance was tinged with sorrow, as Malavika had recently lost the love of her life, just a year prior. Vedant faced with the weight of her grief and the challenges it posed to their relationship.

How Hard can it be?

Vedant often sought solace in his garage, a sanctuary of sorts where he could immerse himself in his work, he has a separate space in the garage to work on his projects. His father had allocated him limited workers, understanding the bustling nature of his business and despite the constraints, Vedant managed skillfully, navigating the intricacies of his craft.

Vedant bought Mumbai's classic Premier Padmini taxi, fondly known as the "kaali-peeli." These taxis, once ubiquitous on the streets, have now become a rarity. Vedant's motivation behind acquiring one was simple: he intended to fashion a rough replica of the iconic Aston Martin DB5 for Malavika. Pouring over blueprints, drawings, photographs and sometimes the internet, Vedant meticulously planned the transformation of the taxi.

His vision was clear, strip away the four-door configuration, elongate the body from the front and the back tail lights are almost similar, he has to chop half the roof from behind and seamlessly merge the roofline with the trunk. The process involved extensive modifications, including refurbishing the engine, a task delegated to a specialized department under Vedant's supervision.

In his workspace, the air hummed with the sounds of chopping, welding, hammering, and the meticulous shaping of metal. Vedant poured his heart and soul into every detail, driven by his love for Malavika and the desire to create something truly extraordinary for her, a testament to the depth of his affection and the lengths he was willing to go to bring her joy.

As Vedant toiled away on his work, Rukmini arrived for a surprise visit. Standing at the gates, she waved eagerly at him. Vedant approached her with a curious smile.

"I see that you're making progress with the car," Rukmini observed. "I wished I could see you finish."

"You can come here every day and see me complete this project," Vedant offered with a hint of pride.

Rukmini smiled wistfully. "Actually, I am here to say goodbye. I am leaving for Kerala today, and I wanted to meet you before I left."

"You're leaving?" Vedant's surprise was evident.

"Yes, I'll be leaving late in the evening. Malavika will drop me," Rukmini confirmed.

"I'll come too," Vedant promptly suggested.

But Rukmini shook her head. "No, you keep working on your project. Finish it as fast as you can."

With a sense of understanding, Vedant nodded. Rukmini then retrieved a camera roll from her pocket and handed it to him.

"I couldn't develop these because I didn't have the time. I am sure you'll find someone to develop these photographs for you," she explained.

Vedant gratefully accepted the roll and stashed it away. Rukmini went on, "I have taken some pictures of you and Malavika while you were not watching. Hope it has come out nice."

A warm smile spread across Vedant's face at the thought. Rukmini then shared her plans, "I am going back to my parents' house. I may settle down and get married there."

"Don't forget to invite me," Vedant insisted earnestly. "I want to be there at your wedding."

Rukmini's smile grew wider as she hugged Vedant affectionately. With a final wave goodbye, she departed, leaving Vedant with a mix of emotions swirling within him.

Later that night, as Vedant made his way home on his bike, a thought occurred to him. He decided to take a detour and have a peek at Malavika's house. Parking his bike across the street, he strolled towards her bungalow's gates. Upon reaching them, he noticed that her door was locked.

"She must have not returned yet," Vedant mused to himself.

Little did he know, Malavika was right behind him. With a mischievous tone, she whispered, "Are you waiting for me?"

Startled, Vedant jumped, and Malavika couldn't help but burst into laughter. "Did I scare you?" she teased.

Recovering from the surprise, Vedant replied, "Yes... I mean no, I was just checking if you're back from the station."

Malavika smiled knowingly and revealed, "She took a flight; I went to the airport to drop her off."

"Oh," Vedant responded, feeling a tad embarrassed.

Sensing Vedant's hesitation, Malavika offered, "Do you want to come in?"

Declining politely, Vedant said, "No, it's getting late. I better leave. Besides, you must be tired."

Admitting her fatigue, Malavika suggested, "Yes, I am tired. Would you like to have a drink with me? I'm not a regular drinker, but today I feel like having one, and I hate drinking alone."

Accepting her invitation, Vedant asked, "Okay, do you want me to get a bottle from outside? I haven't seen you have any at your place."

Chuckling, Malavika revealed, "I have a whole bar you haven't seen yet. Come, let me show you something."

Leading Vedant inside, Malavika guided him to the basement. Vedant was surprised. "You have a basement?"

"Yes, I've been renovating it, and Rukmini has helped me a lot to finish the interior of this room," Malavika explained.

With curiosity piqued, Vedant followed Malavika downstairs, where another door awaited. Opening it and flicking on the lights, Malavika revealed what lay beyond.

Vedant couldn't believe his eyes when he stepped into the room; it was like stepping back in time to the 70s. The vibrant colors of the sofa, the fluffy white carpet, the disco ball hanging from the ceiling, the retro bar stocked with bottles, the jukebox, and even a pinball machine, it was a blast from the past. Malavika led Vedant to a wardrobe bursting with 70s fashion: flashy party wear, sparkling Jewelry, groovy shoes, and funky sunglasses.

Vedant's gaze landed on a stack of vinyl records next to the wardrobe. "You have music records?" he asked incredulously.

"And an LP player," Malavika confirmed.

"You have a player and a jukebox," Vedant remarked.

"Yeah, Manu preferred the jukebox, and I wanted an LP player, so I got both," Malavika explained.

"Manu?" Vedant inquired.

"Manoj... we always dreamed of having a 70s-style room together. Since he's no longer with us, I decided to create this space in his memory," Malavika revealed, her voice tinged with emotion.

Vedant was touched by her gesture. "Why don't you choose an album? Let's play some music," she suggested.

Vedant quickly scanned the records and picked out a classic 70s English rock band. "Interesting choice," Malavika remarked.

"Well, they have elements of glam rock and influenced early English punk music," Vedant explained.

Malavika raised her eyebrows and said, "Whatever... why don't you just play it?"

As the music filled the room, Malavika guided Vedant to the wardrobe. "This side is men's clothing, and this side is women's. Let me choose something you'll never wear in your life," she said mischievously.

Vedant was already sporting a solid black shirt. Malavika handed him a shimmering gold-colored short jacket to wear over it. She unbuttoned two top buttons of his shirt, slightly revealing his bare chest, and then slipped the jacket over him, leaving it unzipped. Next, she searched for a pair of trousers and presented Vedant with a flare bottom dark blue matte finish trousers.

"How is this?" she asked, displaying the trousers.

Vedant hesitated for a moment before accepting them. "I guess I should try them," he said.

"I have a bathroom in here; you can change there," Malavika offered.

As Vedant headed to the bathroom, Malavika seized the opportunity to select her own outfit. She chose a pastel light blue, high-waist, flare bottom trouser and paired it with a white, big-collar, full-sleeved shirt to be tucked inside. Since Vedant was taking too long just to wear a pair of trousers, Malavika headed up to her bedroom and quickly changed into her 70s outfit. Adding a touch of nostalgia, she applied pop-up blue eyeshadow and shimmering light pink lip color.

When she returned to the basement, Vedant was busy preparing drinks. He looked up and was stunned by Malavika's transformation. He couldn't take his eyes off her, and Malavika was equally impressed by Vedant's attire.

Vedant walked up to Malavika and handed her a glass of drink.

Malavika took a big gulp from her drink and then stared at Vedant.

"Do you wanna dance?" Vedant asked her.

Malavika nodded her head, and as the song changed, they slowly began to groove to the music. Before they knew it, they had been dancing for hours, completely losing track of time and enjoying several drinks along the way.

Eventually, Vedant felt tired and collapsed onto the furry white carpet. "I am tired," he admitted.

Malavika, a little tipsy herself, laughed at him. "Tired already?" she teased, joining him on the carpet.

"This is the best soft carpet ever," she exclaimed, lying down beside Vedant.

They closed their eyes, just listening to the music, and enjoyed the moment together.

When Vedant opened his eyes, something felt off. The music had stopped, and there was an eerie silence. Checking his watch, he realized it was 9:30 in the morning. Panic surged through him, and he quickly got up.

Beside him, Malavika still slept, undisturbed by his movements. He attempted to wake her, but she remained unresponsive. Vedant decided to leave her there and make a swift exit.

As he stepped out of the house, the sunlight hit his face, even the mild 9:30 sun felt too bright. Shielding his eyes with his hand, he hurried to the gate. Across the road, he found his bike and sped home.

Arriving at his house, Vedant found the main door open. Inside, he spotted his parents seated at the dining table and they were having their breakfast, they both looked at him in disbelief. Trying to play it cool, Vedant quietly made his way to his room. However, his mom called out to him, prompting him to step back into the living area.

"What are you wearing?" his mom asked, her eyes wide with surprise.

Vedant's own eyes widened as he slowly looked down at his attire. "Oh, shit," he muttered, realizing his blunder. He hurried back into his room without saying a word.

Watching her son's hasty retreat, Vedant's mom turned to his dad. "This doesn't look good. Why is he dressed like a male prostitute?" she whispered anxiously.

Vedant's dad laughed at her concern. "Relax," he said between bites of breakfast. "He probably went to a costume party. But just to ease your mind, I'll ask him about it at work. So, chillax and have your breakfast."

It was afternoon, and Vedant was back in his garage, fully engrossed in his project. As he worked, one of his employees approached him and said, "A madam waiting for you over there," pointing towards Malavika standing outside the garage at a distance. Vedant quickly entered the office cabin, retrieved a bag from the locker, and dashed towards her.

Malavika was clad in a saree, looking absolutely stunning. Vedant stood there, momentarily entranced by her beauty, until Malavika snapped her fingers, bringing him back to reality. He handed over the bag to her, whispering, "It's the jacket and the trousers. I took good care of it."

Accepting the bag, Malavika took a peek inside the garage, where Vedant's project car was taking shape. Without a word, she walked straight in, much to Vedant's panic. He tried to stop her, but she reached his workstation.

Malavika looked at the car, recognizing the rough skeleton of an Aston Martin DB5. Her expression turned serious as she turned to Vedant and asked, "What is this?"

Vedant hesitated, explaining that it was for a client.

Malavika pressed further, questioning "Your client asked for a DB5 replica?" Nervously, Vedant laughed and attempted to clarify, but Malavika walked out on him.

Vedant followed her until she stepped out of the garage, calling out to her. Malavika stopped and turned back, walking towards him. Vedant remained silent, unsure of what to say. Malavika broke the silence, asking, "Did you have lunch yet?"

Vedant shook his head. "No."

Taking charge, Malavika led Vedant to a nearby restaurant. Vedant was nervous; he didn't say much. Malavika ordered food for both of them without even asking Vedant what he would like.

"I am sorry I didn't ask you what you would like," Malavika said, realizing her oversight.

"I am okay with what you ordered, but you don't seem okay, is something wrong?" Vedant responded.

Lunch was served, and while they were eating, Malavika spoke up, "I made you wear Manoj's clothes because I missed him. I'm sorry, I used you to make me feel better." She paused for a moment, gathering her thoughts. "I know you have a crush on me. Even though I liked the idea of a guy liking me, I'm not ready for this. Plus, you're very young, and you'll soon find someone younger and more beautiful. You know that, don't you? I can't do this because it's difficult for me. I want to stay alone for a while, and that's why I moved in here."

Vedant sat there in shock, unable to utter a word. Malavika continued, "I think you should stop coming to my place. It would be better for both of us." With that, she left the restaurant, leaving Vedant behind.

Lost for words, Vedant sat there alone, trying to process what just happened. He hadn't expected things to take such a sudden turn. As he sat there, he couldn't help but wonder what went wrong.

Samrat, aged 28, His parents had arranged a meeting with Varsha, a 27-year-old girl. It was the typical Indian tale of arranged marriage, a concept he never quite warmed up to, so he rejected Varsha, but he found himself in a situation he never quite imagined. Now he wants to marry the same girl.

how hard can it be?

As Samrat's phone buzzed with Varsha's message, he felt a rush of anticipation. "Please come to the corner coffee shop in an hour, I have something important to say," her words echoed in his mind, stirring a mix of excitement and nerves within him.

"What could it possibly be?" Samrat mused, his thoughts racing. Was Varsha about to end things with Vinod, or was this the dreaded farewell he had feared?

Caught in a whirlwind of emotions, Samrat juggled his duties at work with the urgency of Varsha's summons. With determination, he approached his boss and negotiated an extension to his lunch break, eager to heed Varsha's call.

Leaving the restaurant behind, Samrat made his way to the coffee shop, each step heavy with anticipation. The air crackled with uncertainty as he pushed open the door, the aroma of coffee mingling with the weight of impending revelation, his mind raced with thoughts. He wasn't sure what she wanted to tell him, but he hoped it wasn't what he feared most, that she was going to bid him farewell for good.

As always, Varsha was already there when Samrat arrived. She sat quietly, nursing her coffee, a picture of serenity. Samrat couldn't help but admire her, even in the midst of his turmoil.

"Come sit, what will you have?" Varsha asked Samrat, her voice gentle yet tinged with an air of heaviness.

"I just had my lunch, I'll have a soft drink," Samrat replied, trying to mask his nerves.

As he sat down, Varsha's quiet demeanor only added to his anxiety. He feared the worst – that she was about to deliver news that would shatter him completely.

"My wedding is fixed with Vinod; I am getting married in two weeks' time," Varsha finally spoke, her words hitting Samrat like a ton of bricks.

Samrat felt a lump form in his throat as he struggled to process the information. He took a sip of his drink, trying to compose himself.

"So you called me here to give me this news?" Samrat managed to utter, his voice betraying the turmoil within him.

"I was about to call you on the phone first, but I had to show you something before leaving this place," Varsha explained, her eyes betraying a hint of sadness.

Despite his own heartbreak, Samrat couldn't help but feel a pang of sympathy for Varsha. He knew she was caught in the same web of expectations and traditions as he was.

"What is it?" he asked, his voice softening with compassion.

Varsha guided Samrat to a peculiar spot, and as they arrived, Samrat halted his bike across the street. On the opposite side stood a modest-looking small bungalow, its simplicity veiled by the charm of two gates. One gate led to the bungalow itself, while the other, adjacent to the bungalow, opened onto a road spacious enough for a car to pass through. This road wound its way to the backyard of the bungalow, a secluded space shielded by fencing, inaccessible from the outside.

With a gentle gesture, Varsha beckoned Samrat to bring his bike inside through the second gate. As they entered, a narrow path unfolded before them, leading towards the lush green expanse of the backyard. The air was thick with the scent of freshly cut grass, and the sight of the sprawling lawn was a soothing balm to their senses.

But it was what lay beyond the lawn that truly captivated them. Nestled in the corner of the backyard stood a magnificent 'L'-shaped studio apartment, its architecture a testament to beauty and grace.

Samrat couldn't help but marvel at the sight before him, his eyes tracing the contours of the structure with wonder. It was as if this hidden gem had been waiting for them, a secret sanctuary tucked away from the chaos of the world.

Samrat parked his bike to the side, and as he did, the owner of the bungalow, an elderly man, peered over the fence and called out to Varsha.

"Aree beta, you're getting married in 15 days, what are doing here? Don't you have preparations to do for the wedding?" he inquired.

Varsha smiled warmly and replied, "Yes Uncle, I am here only for a short while."

From inside the house, Uncle's wife could be heard calling him, prompting him to bid Varsha a hasty farewell. "Okay beta, take care, I gotta go inside; your aunty is cooking and she needs help," he explained before disappearing indoors.

Varsha led Samrat to one end of the apartment, where a small door beckoned from behind. With a set of keys in hand, Varsha unlocked the door and ushered Samrat inside. The room was cozy, filled with an array of artwork and paintings adorning the walls. An artist's desk and a separate computer desk occupied one corner, while shelves brimming with paint bottles, brushes, crayons, pencils, and various other artist supplies crowded one another.

Samrat surveyed the room with wide-eyed wonder, his gaze lingering on the intricate paintings displayed before him. "I didn't know you painted as well," he remarked, genuinely surprised by Varsha's hidden talent. Varsha nodded, a hint of pride in her voice as she explained, "I do this as a hobby, but I earn money from the manga I work on."

As Samrat took in the sight of Varsha's creations, he couldn't help but feel a newfound admiration for her. Here was a woman of many talents, whose creativity knew no bounds. As he stood amidst her artwork, he kept wondering why is she showing me all this.

There was an abundance of small artworks, enough to cover the entire wall of the 'L'-shaped studio apartment. Varsha pulled out a graphic novel from the drawer and then handed Samrat her novel.

"Read it when you're alone, it's the last adult Manga I worked on," she instructed.

Samrat examined the book, flipping through the pages until something caught his eye. With a surprised raise of his eyebrows and a smirk, he glanced back at Varsha.

"Save it for later," she said, interrupting his curiosity, "and now pay attention to what I have to say."

Samrat tucked the novel behind his jeans, his focus now on Varsha's words.

"This is my workshop," she began, "I've been coming here for three years, working secretly on my adult manga. And when I'm not working on projects, I indulge in painting and other art forms. My parents think I work in a call center; they know nothing about my secret life."

"Why didn't you tell them?" Samrat inquired.

Varsha sighed, her gaze distant as she replied, "It's never easy for a girl. But at least I followed my dreams and did what I wanted, even if it was only for a short time."

"Now you're giving up everything for marriage," Samrat remarked solemnly.

Varsha nodded with a sense of resignation in her voice. "I have to get married someday. Anyway, I want you to take care of my place when I'm gone. I pay rent to Uncle and Aunty for this space, and since they haven't been able to find any tenants, I've decided to continue paying them until they do. Their livelihood depends on it."

"And when they do find someone, where will I put all your artwork?" Samrat questioned.

Varsha shrugged, a hint of sadness in her expression. "I don't know. I don't need them anymore. I'm sure you'll think of something."

As they stood amidst the remnants of Varsha's secret world, Samrat couldn't help but feel a pang of sadness. Yet, he also felt a sense of responsibility, knowing that he would carry a piece of Varsha's dreams with him, even as she embarked on a new chapter of her life.

Samrat and Varsha stepped outside, and Varsha locked the door before handing over the keys to Samrat. "Can we take a look inside the rest of the place?" Samrat suggested.

Varsha nodded, "Yes, it's empty. The door isn't locked." With curiosity driving them, they explored the entirety of the 'L'-shaped studio apartment.

Varsha explained, "This is almost a 3000 square feet area, and I've only occupied 100 square feet, like a 10 by 10 size room in that corner. Nobody wants to rent it as a house; it's more suitable for an office or something. But I love the front yard. Imagine if this were a hidden restaurant, with tables and chairs outside and inside as well, like the one we once visited."

Samrat was struck with inspiration, visualizing the potential of the space as a bustling restaurant. Lost in his thoughts, Varsha gently held his hands, bringing him back to reality. Samrat looked at her, and she spoke softly, "I had fun getting to know you. You were the only person I shared my secret with."

Samrat faced her, his expression somber. "I wish you weren't getting married," he confessed.

Varsha sighed, "But I am."

Samrat's disappointment lingered, and he asked, "You didn't invite me?"

Varsha hesitated before replying, "I guess it would be awkward for both of us."

Samrat stood there, lost in contemplation. Varsha broke the silence, "It's time, Samrat."

Samrat smiled sadly, realizing that this would be the last time he dropped Varsha home. With a heavy heart, he bid her farewell, knowing that their paths were now destined to diverge.

FIVE

THE KIDNAPPERS VAN.

After leaving Varsha's home, Samrat had to rush back to work. It was already too late; he had been away for hours. When he finally returned to the restaurant, his boss erupted like a volcano, blasting Samrat with a tirade of anger. Despite his best efforts, Samrat struggled to maintain his composure as his boss continued to nag him relentlessly.

Eventually, Samrat couldn't take it anymore and snapped, "Stop! I've heard enough of you. I quit." With those words, he stormed out of the restaurant, leaving his boss speechless behind.

Samrat revved up his bike and sped straight to Nikhil's house. As he arrived, he spotted Priya standing in the corridor, lost in thought. Samrat couldn't help but wonder if she was the same girl Nikhil was enamored with.

Priya turned to look at Samrat, and he quickly averted his gaze, focusing on ringing Nikhil's doorbell. Priya retreated into her house as Samrat watched her disappear inside.

Nikhil opened the door, clearly surprised to see Samrat at this hour. "Come in," he called out, inviting Samrat into his home.

Samrat said, "I just saw your girlfriend; she was hanging out in the corridor."

Nikhil, avoiding eye contact with Samrat, replied, "We're not on talking terms anymore. Her mother has asked me to stay away from her."

Samrat didn't know how to respond. He sat down quietly, lost in thought. Sensing his friend's distress, Nikhil asked, "What's wrong?"

With a heavy heart, Samrat confessed, "Varsha is getting married in two weeks, and I quit my job at the restaurant."

Nikhil's eyes widened in shock. "What?" he exclaimed.

"I didn't know what else to do, so I came here," Samrat explained.

Nikhil shook his head, realizing the gravity of the situation. "You're in a bigger mess than I am."

Samrat and Nikhil sat on their apartment balcony and poured their hearts out to each other. Nikhil shared his side of the story, and Samrat did the same. As they exchanged their experiences, they both felt a weight lifted off their shoulders.

Nikhil said, "You always said you wanted a restaurant of your own. Have you saved any money yet?"

Samrat replied, "Yes, I have. But what are you talking about?"

"You should rent out that place and open a restaurant there," Nikhil suggested.

Samrat hesitated, saying, "It's not as easy as you think."

Nikhil persisted, "Well, like you said, the place is ready. All you have to do is get a kitchen installed."

Samrat sighed, conceding, "You're right. But there's a lot of other work that goes into opening a restaurant. I've been working in one for so many years now. I know the trouble of building a restaurant."

Nikhil nodded, acknowledging the challenge. "I guess you're right. Easier said than done."

"We should go out for dinner and maybe have a couple of beers," Samrat suggested.

Nikhil agreed, "Yeah, let's pick Vedant as well."

So Samrat and Nikhil headed out to Vedant's place. On reaching his house, Vedant's dad said, "He is still in the garage. I guess he is working too hard on that car. He might pull an all-nighter."

Deciding to catch Vedant at his garage, they made their way there. As they arrived, they saw Vedant sitting all alone in front of his car.

Nikhil and Samrat looked at the car and were impressed. The car was in bare metal, with the four doors gone, it now had only two doors. It stood on orange-colored temporary spare tires, the engine gleaming like it was brand new. Inside, there was no interior, just an open dashboard with wires dangling all over the place.

Nikhil picked up a photograph of an Aston Martin DB5 lying on a table next to the car. He examined the picture and then looked back at the car, saying, "Wow, you have done an incredible job. It almost looks similar. In fact, once it's completely done, it might look just like the one in the picture."

Samrat came closer and took a look at the picture.

Vedant said, "I was building this car for Malavika. It's one of her favorite cars."

Nikhil responded, "Well, you won my heart. I guess she will go crazy when she sees it."

Vedant's expression shifted as he revealed, "She broke up with me. She said she's not ready for a relationship and thinks I'm too young for her."

Samrat sighed, "Oh no... you too."

Vedant turned to Samrat, curious. "What do you mean?"

Nikhil jumped in, "I lost my girl, and he lost his job and his girl."

Surprised, Vedant asked, "What happened?"

"Can we first have some dinner? I am famished," Samrat interjected.

Nikhil agreed, "We'll tell you our story over dinner. First, let's go eat."

Vedant suggested, "I know a dhaba that remains open till late in the night. They also serve drinks; It's not far from here. We should go there."

Nikhil said, "We didn't bring our bikes."

Vedant reassured them, "No worries, I have just the right vehicle in mind."

Leading them inside the garage, Vedant unveiled a yellow-colored van. Though the paint was old and chipped in some places, Vedant had clear coated the entire van, making it shine like a brand-new vehicle.

Except for the driver's end, the rest of the van had no windows. "The Kidnappers Van" was highlighted in large font, the words spray-painted in bold red color in a graffiti-style art on the vehicle.

Samrat was curious, "Where did you get this from?"

Vedant explained, "I made it for a customer. It was his idea. He wanted this van to look exactly like this, but he backed out in the middle due to some money crisis. But then I decided to finish it, and here it is. I call it the Kidnappers Van, and this is officially my van now."

Vedant went to the back of the van and opened the double doors from behind. Inside, it was all empty except for three bean bags casually dumped inside. "Get in, you're gonna enjoy this ride," Vedant invited.

Nikhil eagerly jumped in and threw himself at one of the bean bags, followed by Samrat. Vedant shut the double doors and settled into the driver's seat at the front. Glancing back, he asked, "How is it back there?"

"Awesome, now let's go. I am famished," Samrat replied eagerly.

Vedant drove the van out and headed towards the dhaba he had mentioned.

At the dhaba, they were so hungry that they ended up ordering more food than they could possibly eat. The dhaba also served beer, adding to the relaxed atmosphere.

As they ate, they slowly started sharing their experiences one by one. Soon, all three of them knew each other's half-baked love stories.

After the meal, they headed back to the van. Parked next to an open field, they were a little tipsy from the drinks. The wind rustled through the field, and the clear night sky glowed in the darkness, illuminated by the moonlight.

Vedant said, "I am not going anywhere." He pulled the back double door wide open, then entered and buried himself on the bean bag, facing outward towards the open fields shining in the moonlight.

Nikhil and Samrat joined him, sitting facing outside. The wind outside blew coolly, sending a refreshing breeze into the van.

For a while, there was silence. Then Nikhil broke it, "Is it wrong to fall in love with a younger girl?"

Vedant and Samrat responded in unison, "Yes if she is a teenager." They exchanged amused glances and burst into laughter.

Nikhil defended, "Come on... she is 19."

Samrat chimed in ironically, "How ironic? You should be dating someone like Malavika, and you, Vedant, should be dating someone like Priya."

Vedant added, "And what about you? Even though you had this perfect girl all ready, a match made in heaven, I mean a match made by your mom, yet you managed to screw everything."

Nikhil intervened, "Let it be, Yaar. Don't be too hard on him."

The three of them fell silent again, staring out into the night. After a few more minutes, Vedant broke the silence.

Vedant looked at Samrat and said, "You do realize that you have two weeks to win her back."

Samrat stared back, incredulous. "Are you crazy?" he replied.

Nikhil, confused, asked, "What do you mean?"

Vedant explained, "What do you do when you propose to a girl?"

Samrat replied, "You give her a ring."

"Exactly," Vedant affirmed. "My 'ring' is the car I am building. I know gifting a car can seem like showing off, and there's a saying that any girl would love a car as a gift. But Malavika is different and besides I'm not buying her a car; I'm building her one. I'm putting everything into it, pouring all my love into this build. So, I've decided that I'll finish building this car in a week's time, and instead of a ring, I'll present her with this car and propose to her."

Nikhil pondered, "You think she'll accept your proposal?"

"That's the thing," Vedant replied with determination. "If I don't try, how will I know?"

Samrat said, "Sounds like a plan, but what will I do?"

Nikhil suggested, "Rent that place and turn it into a restaurant."

Vedant nodded in agreement, "Yes, once you're done, call her and show her the restaurant. Tell her you want to marry her and settle down."

Samrat voiced his concern, "You think she'll call off her wedding?"

Vedant replied confidently, "If you give her enough time. That's why I'm telling you, you have to finish building that restaurant in a week, leaving her a good week's time to think."

Samrat shook his head, feeling overwhelmed. "This all sounds like too much. Are we drunk?"

Vedant reassured him, "No, it's just the breeze. We both have one week to win our girls back."

Determined, Samrat agreed, "I agree; I am ready for this challenge."

Nikhil added, "You guys are right. Priya told me this. She prefers a guy who fights for his girl and doesn't give up."

Samrat couldn't help but remark, "Frankly, it's easy for you. All you need to do is be firm and you can make her your girlfriend. That is if you don't care what her mother thinks."

Nikhil fell into a deep thought, and silence enveloped the van once again. The night was beautiful, accompanied by the faint sound of old Hindi movie songs playing in the nearby dhaba.

Samrat called out to Vedant and said, "Can I borrow your van? I might need it to get stuff for the restaurant."

Vedant replied, "No problem, you can use my van."

"I'll need to arrange manpower to start the work. I wonder how I'll advertise my restaurant?" Samrat mused.

Vedant looked at Nikhil and said, "I have an idea. You can also score brownie points with Priya."

Nikhil, intrigued, asked, "How?"

Vedant explained, "Priya is a vlogger, right? And she has many followers on her social network?"

Nikhil nodded, "Yes."

"Plus, she has this college project where she wants to do a documentary film, right?" Vedant continued.

"Yes," Nikhil confirmed.

"Samrat is the answer to all your prayers. You go tomorrow and call her. Tell her your friend Samrat is building a restaurant in a week, and she can document the whole thing from start to finish. Not only that, she can also do her vlogs and post videos on her social media page. By doing that, Samrat will get free marketing for his restaurant from her," Vedant suggested.

Samrat, excited, exclaimed, "That's an amazing idea!"

Nikhil chimed in, "That is an awesome idea. Thanks, Vedant."

Vedant struggled to get up from the bean bag, eventually managing to stand. He said, "Thank me when things actually work out for us. But for now, I need to pee." With that, Vedant walked out of the van to relieve himself. He stood at the edge of the field, with Samrat and Nikhil joining him.

"I can't wait for the sun to rise. Now I know what I am going to do first thing in the morning," Nikhil remarked.

"Me too," Samrat agreed.

"Me three," Vedant added with a chuckle.

After they had finished, Vedant safely drove the van and dropped Samrat and Nikhil home.

The next morning, Nikhil woke up feeling a little dizzy. Knowing it was Saturday and he didn't have to go to the office, he headed straight to the bathroom and turned on the shower. As the water cascaded down, he couldn't help but remember everything that had happened the night before.

After his shower, Nikhil brushed his teeth, had a clean shave, and dressed himself. Determined, he decided he was going to talk to Priya. Stepping out of his flat, he rang the doorbell of his neighbor's house. Despite feeling nervous, he knew Priya's mom would likely answer the door, so he prepared himself to face her.

When Priya's mom opened the door, she was surprised to see Nikhil. "What is it?" she asked.

Nikhil replied, "Is Priya home? I have something important to say."

Priya's mom responded, "What is it? Tell me, and I'll give her the message when she returns from college."

Nikhil checked his watch in surprise, then looked back at Priya's mom. "Oh, it's late. She already left. Never mind, I'll tell her myself." With that, he turned and left. Priya's mother watched him go, wondering what was it all about.

Nikhil was in the midst of taking his scooter out when his phone rang. It was Samrat, asking him to meet up at Vedant's garage. Upon arrival, Nikhil spotted Vedant and Samrat waiting for him inside the van.

"Park your scooter inside my garage and hop in," Vedant instructed.

"I'm off to Priya's college to meet her," Nikhil responded.

"She'll be in class right now. We'll go later. First, we'll make a stop at Samrat's new restaurant place," Vedant suggested.

Nikhil agreed and parked his scooter inside the garage before joining them in the van.

Half an hour later, Nikhil, Samrat, and Vedant were sitting on the couch, sipping tea, with the elderly couple sitting across from them.

Uncle inquired, "You want to rent the whole place?"

Samrat nodded, replying, "Yes."

Aunty interjected, "Beta, your idea of opening a restaurant is not good. This place is hidden, and that's why we don't get any offers. I think you should reconsider."

Uncle added, "Yes, I think she's right. Besides, you can ask your friend Varsha. I'm sure she'll tell you the same."

The three friends exchanged glances, and then Samrat spoke up, "Uncle, please don't tell Varsha about this yet. This is a secret project."

Uncle and Aunty looked at each other. Aunty then asked, "How will you pay the rent? You won't do business right from the start."

Vedant chimed in, suggesting, "How about profit sharing then? Samrat is confident the restaurant will do well in the future."

Samrat agreed, "Yes, profit sharing looks like a good idea. Initially, you will get less money than expected, but I am sure later you'll get more money than the rent you have in mind."

Uncle and Aunty exchanged glances before stating they needed to discuss. Samrat, Vedant, and Nikhil stepped out of the bungalow to give them some privacy.

After a few minutes, Uncle and Aunty emerged, agreeing to the deal. Uncle said, "You can start working today if you want. The doors to the studio apartment are open. If you need any help, let me know."

Samrat expressed his gratitude, saying, "Thanks, Uncle, and thanks, Aunty."

Uncle remarked, "I am only doing this because you are Varsha's friend. I think you should apply for a license straight away, and we can do all the paperwork tomorrow morning."

As Samrat, Vedant, and Nikhil exited the gate and entered the area next to the bungalow, they reached the backyard of the elderly couple's bungalow and gazed at the property, Uncle peeped over the fence and urged them, "Don't just stand there admiring the place. If you have to complete it in one week, you better get started."

Aunty called from inside, prompting Uncle to say, "My wife is cooking; I've got to go."

Vedant handed over the keys to Samrat and said, "You can use the van." Samrat hugged Vedant gratefully.

"That's all the help you will get from me; I have to work on my car," Vedant added.

Samrat nodded understandingly. "No worries, Nikhil is there to help."

Nikhil chimed in, "Only for two days. I have a 9 to 6 job; I'm not a business guy like you two. But I'll come every day after work to help."

Samrat smiled appreciatively. "I know why you'll come to help—because Priya will be here, that's why. Speaking of which, have you talked to Priya yet?"

Nikhil realized his scooter was back at the garage. "Let's go get that first. Then I can go to her college and wait for her there."

Vedant suggested, "Why wait? Call her now and tell her to come out as soon as her current lecture is over. Tell her we will be waiting outside the gate with our van."

Nikhil immediately sent her a text message.

They parked the van in front of the college gates, and Nikhil, Vedant, and Samrat waited outside next to it. Vedant asked, "Did she reply?"

Nikhil shook his head. "No, but she has read the message."

As they waited, a security guard left his post and began walking toward them. Samrat whispered, "Is he walking towards us?"

Vedant squinted. "Looks like it."

Nikhil's heart sank. "Oh no."

Vedant asked, "What's wrong?"

Nikhil explained, "It's your van. It says 'The Kidnappers Van,' and we've parked it right in front of a college. He's going to call the police."

Vedant scoffed. "Are you nuts?"

Samrat suggested, "I think we should leave."

Vedant shook his head. "If we run, they'll surely think we're kidnappers. Let me handle this."

The security guard approached them, eyeing the van. Then, he looked back at them and said, "How much do you charge for kidnapping?"

Vedant was taken aback. "Excuse me?"

The security guard laughed. "Since you've advertised your work so well, I thought I should make a little fun of it. Anyway, what are you guys doing here?"

Vedant replied quickly, "We're waiting for our sister."

The guard raised an eyebrow. "Your sister studies here?"

Vedant nodded. "Yes."

The guard glanced at them suspiciously before saying, "Hmmm," and walking back to his post.

A little while later, Priya arrived at the gate with three of her friends. The guard stopped them, his expression stern. "Those three morons are here for you? Do you know them? One of them lied to my face, saying he was waiting for his sister."

Priya chuckled softly. "Sister? Well... I know them, so you don't have to worry. Besides, I am taking my three bodyguards along." With that, Priya and her three friends walked confidently toward the van.

Priya positioned herself at the front, while her three friends stood behind her, exuding an air of protection.

Nikhil, Samrat, and Vedant were standing together, Nikhil stepped forward and addressed Priya, "Priya, I have something important to say. Will you step inside the van with me for a moment?"

Samrat interjected nervously, "Are you crazy? The guard is still watching us." Everyone turned back and glanced at the guard, and Samrat squeaked and whispered, "Don't look at him; he'll think something's fishy."

Vedant tried to calm Samrat down. "Samrat, don't get too worked up. Relax."

Nikhil insisted, "I need privacy. I'll take a walk with Priya. You guys wait here." With that, Nikhil and Priya strolled away, leaving Samrat, Vedant, and Priya's three friends behind.

The three girls who had been standing behind approached Vedant and Samrat. One of them remarked to Vedant, "I've seen you before, but I can't recollect where."

Samrat quickly chimed in, "He went to the same college. Probably you must have known him from there."

Vedant's face turned red, and he exchanged a glance with Samrat. Then, one of the other girls exclaimed loudly, "Venky?" She recognized Vedant.

The other two girls also recalled, "Venky, I still have your notes with me."

"Venky, you look good, Yaar," another girl added.

Vedant glanced at Samrat, who was struggling to contain his laughter. "Venky?" Samrat managed to say amidst his amusement.

Meanwhile, Nikhil and Priya were taking a leisurely walk. Nikhil halted Priya and spoke earnestly, "I know we have a huge age difference, and your mom is not happy about it. But I've made up my mind, and I don't want to lose you. I really do love you, and I want to be with you. I want you to be my girlfriend, and I am serious about what I just said. I want to marry you someday, whenever you're ready."

Priya was taken aback, her eyes welling up with tears. But she smiled, blushed, and then turned pink with happiness. She was rendered speechless, unable to find the right words to respond.

Sensing her overwhelmed state, Nikhil decided to lighten the mood. "I have something else for you. Remember your movie project?"

Priya nodded eagerly. "Yes?"

Nikhil continued, "Well, my friend is opening a restaurant, and he will build this restaurant in just a week. You can document everything from start to end. This could be a very good documentary film."

Priya's eyes sparkled with excitement. "Really? When is he starting?"

Nikhil replied, "From today, I guess. I'll pick you up from home when Samrat is ready." As they walked back to the van, Priya held onto Nikhil's arm, her gaze filled with affection. Nikhil smiled back at her, feeling content.

"I am so happy to be with you," Nikhil confessed.

Priya returned the sentiment, saying, "Yeah, me too."

Upon arrival, Priya returned to her girlfriends, and they all chimed in together, "Bye Venky."

Nikhil, puzzled, questioned, "Venky?"

Samrat burst into laughter, while Vedant addressed him, "Do you want the van or not?"

Nikhil persisted, "Whom were they calling Venky?"

Vedant urged, "Get in the van; let's get out of here."

Later that day, everyone except Vedant gathered at Samrat's new restaurant place. The L-shaped studio apartment was a bit dusty, but the entire structure was new and perfect. Samrat and Nikhil arranged some tables and chairs on the lawn, with the Kidnappers Van parked at a distance. Samrat had hired six interns from his industry: two as chefs to work alongside him, three as waiters, and one as a manager. They were all here to help from the beginning.

Nikhil and Priya were also present, along with Priya's three friends who had come to assist her in shooting the documentary film and her vlog. A little while later, Uncle joined them too. As everyone settled down, Samrat prepared to give his first briefing.

In the briefing, Samrat unfolded his ambitious plans, aiming to accomplish everything within a week.

He remarked, "There isn't much to do, yet there's a whole lot to tackle simultaneously. We won't be meddling with Varsha's workshop area, even though she's kindly handed over the keys, assuring she won't need them anymore. I'm optimistic about her return to her workshop. Firstly, we'll set up the kitchen, followed by crafting both indoor and outdoor dining spaces. Envision a grand canopy outside, adorned with a fresh lawn teeming with lush plants and flower pots. The restaurant's walls will boast charming brick textures, complemented by sleek white panel windows. We'll illuminate the surroundings with two neon signboards—one indoors and the other adorning the entrance gate. Our workers will arrive shortly, initiating the tasks with utmost promptness. We've devised two teams—one dedicated to nocturnal operations and the other to daytime endeavors. The quieter tasks, such as electrical wiring, water piping, painting, and gardening, will be undertaken during the night, while the rest will progress during the day."

As Samrat delved into the technical intricacies, Priya carefully recorded every detail, fulfilling her college project requirements.

After the briefing, Nikhil confided in Priya, sharing all about Samrat and Varsha. Filled with enthusiasm for the plan, Priya expressed her desire to see Varsha's workshop.

Samrat, obliging her curiosity, led Nikhil and Priya to Varsha's sanctuary of creativity. Nikhil and Priya stood in awe at the sight of Varsha's artwork adorning the walls, marveling at her talent.

Priya, brimming with excitement, suggested, "I have an idea to impress Varsha." Curious, Samrat inquired, "How?"

With a gleam in her eyes, Priya proposed, "Why don't we display all her artwork on the walls of the restaurant? We can transform this place into a concept restaurant where people can not only dine but also purchase Varsha's artwork. Additionally, we can invite other artists to showcase and sell their work here, with you taking a commission. That way, you can support artists and earn simultaneously."

Nikhil chimed in, "That's a brilliant idea!"

Samrat, struck by inspiration, exclaimed, "I think I've found the perfect name for my restaurant. It just popped into my head."

Eagerly, Priya asked, "What is it?"

With a smile, Samrat revealed, "Salt Pepper and Art."

A week later,

Samrat finally completed his restaurant, the sight was breathtaking—vibrant lights, captivating colors, a charming garden outside, and a splendid display of artwork adorned the walls. It was a masterpiece, a testament to all the hard work invested. Samrat generously granted everyone a day off to rest and rejuvenate, with a firm reminder to return the next day for the soft launch in the evening.

On the eve of the launch, Samrat meticulously planned for a special gathering exclusively for friends and family. He spent the day sending out invitations, ensuring every detail was perfect. However, amidst the preparations, he made a deliberate choice, not to send an invitation to Varsha. Instead, he devised a surprise plan involving Priya and her friends to personally bring Varsha to the launch party the following day.

As anticipation filled the air, Samrat's excitement soared, eager to witness the joy and surprise that awaited Varsha at the grand unveiling of his labor of love.

The next morning, Samrat, Nikhil, and Priya assembled at the restaurant, ready to kick-start the preparations for the evening's launch party.

Samrat's team, brimming with fresh energy and enthusiasm after their day off, dove into their tasks with fervor.

Amidst the hustle and bustle, Priya shared, "I've posted several videos, and many of my followers are excited. I'm certain they'll visit this place."

Appreciating her support, Samrat replied, "You've been a tremendous help to me. Thanks for everything. But there's one final task I need your assistance with."

Understanding what lay ahead, Priya nodded, "I know I have to pick up Varsha in the evening. But I think I should go now and give her a heads-up. What if she can't make it in the evening? Her wedding is just around the corner; she might be busy."

Nikhil chimed in, "She's right. You should send the invitation right now. Don't delay." With unanimous agreement, Samrat agreed.

Priya, accompanied by her friends, ventured to visit Varsha to invite her to Samrat's inaugural party.

Meanwhile, Samrat and Nikhil, not having heard from Vedant in a while, decided to pay him a visit at his garage. As they arrived, Vedant emerged from his garage, his eyes lighting up at the sight of Samrat and Nikhil.

"I received your invitation, and your restaurant looks fantastic. Congratulations," Vedant exclaimed with genuine excitement.

Curious, Samrat inquired, "When did you see my restaurant?"

Vedant explained, "I follow Priya on social media. She's posted awesome pictures of your restaurant, and I love the name Salt, Pepper + Art. My family and I will be there in the evening."

Nikhil, eager to know about Vedant's project, asked, "How's your project coming along?"

Vedant replied, "I was just about to do something before you dropped by. Wait here; I'll be back in a minute."

As Nikhil and Samrat waited outside, they heard the roar of an engine. Moments later, Vedant emerged driving a stunning car.

Samrat exclaimed, "Wow, it does look like a DB5."

Nikhil added, "That's an awesome replica."

Vedant, beaming with pride, invited them to hop in. "I'm taking it out for the first time, a test drive," Vedant announced.

Excitedly, Nikhil and Samrat climbed into the custom-made replica of an Aston Martin DB5 as Vedant drove off into the streets.

Meanwhile, Priya and her friends returned from delivering the invitation to Varsha, but they brought back unsettling news and anxiously awaited the boys' return.

As Vedant brought the car back to the garage, he eagerly inquired, "So, how was it?"

Nikhil couldn't contain his excitement, exclaiming, "I'm jealous! Malavika is going to adore this."

Samrat, curious about Vedant's plans, asked, "When are you giving her the car?"

Vedant replied with a grin, "Tomorrow. I'm waiting for the cover I ordered. It's a beautiful red-colored satin fabric. It'll arrive by this evening, and tomorrow morning, I'll take the car to her place and surprise her."

Eventually, Vedant, Nikhil, and Samrat made their way back to the restaurant, where Priya was waiting. Upon reaching, Priya rushed towards Samrat and delivered the news, "I have bad news for you."

Samrat's heart sank, and he anxiously queried, "She's not coming?"

Priya said, "She's getting married tomorrow."

Vedant and Nikhil exchanged glances, understanding the gravity of the situation. Samrat, perplexed, uttered, "But her wedding was on Saturday. There are still five more days left."

Priya clarified, "Yes, her wedding got preponed. It's tomorrow." Samrat, feeling devastated, was rendered speechless.

Priya continued, "Varsha said she cannot wait for long at the party, but she's excited about your restaurant and assured that she will definitely come in the evening."

Samrat's heart heavy with sadness, found solace in the comforting words of Nikhil and Vedant. Nikhil, with a reassuring tone, expressed, "I am proud of what you did. I know that it was the adrenaline of trying to get Varsha back that made you finish this restaurant in a week. But take a look at what you just did. I think you did your best. You're going to meet her this evening, so be happy and make this meeting memorable." Vedant echoed his support, saying, "Yeah, we support you in your every decision."

Later in the evening, the restaurant opened its doors to guests, filling the air with music, delectable food, and cheerful faces.

Uncle and Auntie from the next-door bungalow, who were also Samrat's business partners, played the role of gracious hosts.

Samrat, dressed in a head chef's attire, dashed between the kitchen and dining area, ensuring everything ran smoothly.

Vedant arrived with his family, while Nikhil stuck close to Priya. Priya's mother, busy making new friends, kept a watchful eye on Nikhil and Priya simultaneously. Priya's friends, equipped with a movie camera, captured the festivities.

As the evening unfolded, Malavika made a stunning entrance, adorned in a gorgeous shimmering red sequin sari. Vedant, awestruck, hastened to escort her. Observing the scene, Vedant's parents exchanged knowing glances.

Vedant's father remarked, "Vedant has scored big time."

Vedant's mother, slightly perturbed, remarked, "She looks a couple of years older than Vedant."

Vedant's father, unfazed, countered, "Who cares? Look, everyone is looking at her."

"Remember that day he wore a tacky outfit; I am sure she's the one who made him wear that," Vedant's mother remarked.

Vedant's father burst into laughter, then wrapped his arms around her shoulder and guided her away, suggesting, "Let's leave them alone."

Malavika looked at Vedant and said, "I am here only because Samrat insisted a lot. Don't keep any expectations from me; I have not changed my mind."

Vedant smiled warmly and replied, "With your permission, is it okay if I show you around this place? Samrat is kind of busy." Malavika returned his gaze and nodded, indicating her agreement.

Meanwhile, Samrat's mother reveled in the joy of her son's accomplishment, beaming with pride. Priya seized the opportunity to interview Samrat, positioning him against the backdrop of his restaurant. She urged him to share his journey of building this beautiful establishment in just a week, a fitting finale for her documentary film project. As the interview concluded and Samrat rose from his seat, he caught sight of Varsha standing at a distance, a smile adorning her face.

Samrat walked towards Varsha, who exclaimed, "Wow... I don't believe you did this in a week's time." She gazed around the place in awe, while Samrat couldn't take his eyes off her.

"Come, let me show you inside," he invited warmly. Leading her indoors, Samrat proudly showcased her paintings and artwork adorning the walls.

Varsha, overcome with emotion, turned to Samrat and asked, "Why?"

Samrat's gaze softened as he confessed, "Because I love you. I thought you had two weeks before getting married, and I hoped maybe I could convince you not to go through with it. But you gave me a shocker."

Varsha explained, her voice tinged with regret, "It wasn't planned. My fiancé Vinod's leave was cut short; he has to join his company earlier than expected, so the wedding got preponed."

Varsha remained quiet, her eyes scanning the surroundings as she wandered into the kitchen. Spotting a small stool tucked away in the corner, she settled onto it. "Prepare something for me, just one plate and a small portion. I can't wait for long," she requested softly.

Samrat quickly got to work, his culinary skills coming to life in the kitchen. As he busily cooked, Varsha observed him with a sense of admiration.

A few minutes later, Samrat appeared with a plate in his hand. Varsha took it, inhaling the aroma before taking the fork Samrat offered.

"This is my take on linguine with clams," he informed her with a smile. Varsha's face lit up as she took a big bite, savoring the flavors. With widened eyes and a nod of approval, she affirmed, "Wow."

"You liked it?" Samrat inquired eagerly. Varsha replied with a hint of nostalgia, "Wish my mom could have tasted this. She would have gone crazy. It's so good." Finishing her plate, Varsha gratefully accepted a cold beverage from Samrat.

Varsha complimented, "You did great. I love everything about this restaurant. All I can do is wish you all the luck for your future."

Samrat's heart sank as he confessed, "I feel gutted leaving you like this. I wish I could marry you."

Varsha, with a gentle smile, attempted to lighten the mood with a joke. "In that case, like in the movies, you'll have to make a daring entry at my wedding tomorrow and kidnap me," she quipped. Samrat's response was tinged with sarcasm, "Seriously?"

Varsha quickly backtracked, realizing her attempt at humor fell flat. "Okay, that was a bad joke. I was just trying to be funny. I wanted you to laugh. I want you to be happy and move on. I'm sure you'll do great," she clarified, trying to ease the tension.

Despite his sadness, Samrat managed a bittersweet smile as Varsha reached into her purse and pulled out an envelope. Handing it to Samrat, she explained, "This is my wedding invitation. At first, I thought it would be weird, but now I want you to come. The reason I'm giving you this is because I want to be at your wedding as well."

Samrat accepted the invitation with mixed emotions, his heart heavy with longing. Varsha then kissed him on the cheek before bidding farewell and heading back home.

The next day, Vedant rose early, taking a quick shower and dressing himself in a sharp black suit paired with a crisp white shirt. He added a slim black necktie and slipped into his driving gloves. Checking his reflection in the mirror, he pondered aloud, "Do I look like a secret agent?" Satisfied with his appearance, he exited his room, only to bump into his mother, who was in the midst of brushing her teeth. Vedant's mother, toothbrush still in hand, stared at him in surprise as he hastily made his escape.

However, Vedant's father intercepted him at the door, retrieving his newspaper. Upon catching sight of Vedant, he raised an eyebrow and remarked, "You do realize those leather gloves are either worn in winter or when you want to kill someone."

Amused by the observation, Vedant replied, "So I do look like a secret agent?"

Vedant's father, with a hint of sarcasm, commented, "Another one of your fancy dress competitions, I suppose?"

Vedant's mother nodded her head in frustration before returning to the bathroom to continue her dental hygiene routine. With a wry smile, Vedant left the scene, making his way towards his garage.

Upon reaching the garage, Vedant retrieved the package delivered the previous day. Inside was the red car cover he had ordered. With determination, he took the cover and climbed into the car, ready to embark on his mission. Vedant drove off, heading towards Malavika's house.

Upon arriving at her bungalow, Vedant halted the car outside the gates. Stepping out, he opened the gates with utmost care, minimizing any noise. Returning to the car, Vedant maneuvered it inside the compound with remarkable silence, parking it in the center of the front yard. Carefully, he unfurled the cloth and draped it over the vehicle.

However, in his haste to cover the car, Vedant forgot to retrieve the key from inside. With the doors unlocked and the windows down, the car sat vulnerable. Yet, Vedant was too focused on his task to notice, eager to complete the transformation with the beautiful red satin fabric cover.

As Samrat entered the gate of his new restaurant, his eyes fell upon the van parked nearby. "Time to return you to the owner," he mused aloud, referring to his intention to return it to Vedant. Retrieving the keys from his pocket, Samrat made his way towards the van. The van had been a tremendous help to Samrat during the construction of his restaurant. Pausing for a moment, he glanced at the vehicle and read aloud, "The Kidnappers Van."

Suddenly, Varsha's words echoed in his mind, "In that case, like in the movies, you will have to make a daring entry at my wedding tomorrow and kidnap me." Overwhelmed by the memories and emotions, Samrat felt a wave of nausea wash over him. Panic threatened to engulf him, but his chef training kicked in.

Slowly, he steadied himself, taking deep breaths to calm his racing heart. After a few moments of reflection, he made a decision and reached for his phone, dialing Vedant's number.

Back at Malavika's place, she was sound asleep in her bedroom when a mobile ringtone startled her awake. Rubbing her eyes, she made her way to the window to investigate the source of the sound. Down below, Vedant was finishing up covering the car, focused on adjusting one corner while his phone continued to ring. Finally, he answered the call.

From her vantage point, Malavika observed Vedant standing beside the covered car, engaged in conversation on his phone. As Vedant spoke, Malavika's eyes widened in shock at the words she heard.

"Are you out of your mind? You want to kidnap Varsha from her wedding?" Vedant's voice carried up to Malavika's window, leaving her stunned at the unexpected revelation.

Vedant continued, his voice strained with concern, "What if she doesn't want to get kidnapped?" After a moment of silence, Vedant listened intently to Samrat's response before adding,

"Okay, only if she agrees to come with us, we make a move." Another pause ensued before Vedant spoke again, "Dude, I was at Malavika's place. I brought the car here. It was my reveal day... Okay-okay, don't... I'll be there."

Disconnecting the call, Vedant stood in contemplation, weighing his options. He glanced back at the main door and then up at Malavika's bedroom window.

Inside, Malavika quickly moved aside before cautiously returning to observe from her vantage point. As she peered down below, she saw Vedant typing something on his phone.

Suddenly, a message beep on her phone startled her, causing her to momentarily lose her balance. Recovering quickly, she retrieved her phone and saw that Vedant had sent her a message, she refrained from opening it or else Vedant would know that she was awake, she cautiously took another peek outside, but to her surprise, Vedant had already left.

Samrat dialed Nikhil's number next, anxiously outlining his plan over the phone.

As Nikhil listened in disbelief, his jaws dropped. "Dude, it doesn't work this way," he interjected. "You have to first talk to Varsha and ask her if she's ready to come with you. We can't just crash into a wedding and kidnap her."

Samrat insisted, "We'll get there first, and I'll plead with her to come with me. I'll tell her how much I love her and that I want to marry her."

Nikhil voiced his concern, "And if she refuses?"

Samrat remained resolute, "Then we'll return empty-handed, no fuss, I promise. Listen, I'm not going insane, but I have to give this a shot. I have a feeling she'll come with me. Please hurry, I'm waiting at the restaurant."

With a heavy heart, Samrat ended the call, leaving Nikhil troubled by his friend's impulsive decision. Nikhil hurriedly dressed himself and made his way to Priya's house next door.

He rang the doorbell, and Priya's mother answered. Nikhil asked for Priya, and although Priya's mother stared at him with curiosity, she called out for Priya. Priya emerged from her room, noticing Nikhil's worried expression.

"What's wrong?" she asked.

Nikhil wasted no time in expressing his concerns. "It's Samrat. I think he's going to do something stupid, and we have to stop him."

Priya looked confused but determined. "Okay, wait for me down at the parking. I'll quickly change," she assured him.

With a nod, Nikhil headed down to the parking lot, knowing that Priya would join him soon.

A short while later, Nikhil and Priya drove off from their building. Priya, seated behind Nikhil on his scooter, inquired, "Now tell me everything in detail." Nikhil proceeded to narrate Samrat's plan to her.

Meanwhile, at Malavika's residence, she descended from her house and walked to her front yard, where she spotted the car wrapped in a red satin cover. Tempted to unravel it, she hesitated and decided to check the message first. The message read, 'I am sure you must have understood it's a car, but I don't want you to open it till I come back. Because I want to be there when you unravel it, I want to see your face when you'll see the car for the first time and I have a lot to say to you, so please be patient and wait for me. I had to leave urgently, some emergency thing came up.'

Resolving to wait, Malavika returned inside her house, her curiosity piqued and anticipation building for the moment when she would uncover the surprise.

Meanwhile, at the restaurant, Nikhil parked his scooter and approached Vedant and Samrat, followed by Priya.

Nikhil wasted no time expressing his disapproval, stating, "It's a very bad idea."

Vedant echoed Nikhil's sentiment, adding, "I have been telling him that for half an hour now, but he won't listen."

Concerned, Nikhil emphasized the potential consequences, saying, "We could go to jail for this."

Vedant elaborated on the financial repercussions, warning, "Do you know how much a wedding costs? You're going to give her parents a heart attack."

Despite their objections, Samrat remained adamant, challenging them, "Are you in or not?"

Nikhil looked to Priya, urging her to intervene. "Please put some sense into him," he implored.

Priya, taking charge, asked Samrat, "Do you have the wedding invitation?"

Samrat said, 'Yes I do, her wedding is in the evening.' Samrat pulls out the card, handing it over to Priya. As she read the invitation, panic set in.

"The wedding is going to take place right now in the morning. It's the reception that will take place in the evening. We've got to go now," she exclaimed.

The shocking revelation left Nikhil, Vedant, and Samrat in disbelief. Priya, frustrated, urged them into action. "Don't just stand there, we have to go now," she insisted.

Vedant volunteered to drive, while Nikhil, incredulous, muttered, "I don't believe I am doing this."

Samrat, grateful for Priya's presence, tapped Nikhil on the back and said 'Thanks for bringing Priya along.'

Nikhil, retorted, "I brought her to... What the f@#k, let's go."

With urgency, they all piled into the van and sped off towards the wedding destination, uncertainty looming over their impromptu mission.

At Varsha's wedding venue, everything was almost ready. It was an outdoor wedding, with a beautifully decorated podium placed in the center where the ceremony would take place. Colorful flowers adorned the area, and a red carpet aisle led to the gates of the venue. Ice sculptures and large flower vases adorned both sides of the aisle. Guests were seated on either side, enjoying beverages and refreshments while traditional wedding music played softly in the background.

On the podium, the groom sat next to the holy fire, with the Pandit engrossed in his Pooja, chanting mantras. In between, he remarked, 'It's almost time; make sure the bride is ready and she comes on time.'

Varsha, dressed in her bridal attire, was escorted by her family and friends to the podium. As she took her seat, a white van suddenly crashed through the main gate, knocking over decorative flower vases, ice sculptures, and a few chairs. The van screeched to a halt right in front of the podium.

Varsha stood up in shock, a bad feeling washing over her. What if it's Samrat? Her heart raced as she feared that Samrat might have taken her joke seriously. She stared at the van, her apprehension growing with each passing moment.

A group of girls emerged from the van and headed towards the podium. One of the girls stepped forward, approaching Vinod. Vinod, equally shocked, stood up and looked at the girl in disbelief. "Anu?" he exclaimed in surprise.

The girl knelt before Vinod and professed her love for him, expressing her desire to marry him. Vinod, still reeling from the unexpected turn of events, managed to respond, "You rejected me before, and now on the wedding day, you're causing a scene."

Tears streamed down the girl's cheeks as she stood up, admitting that she had come to her senses. She acknowledged Vinod's love for her and pleaded with him to run away with her, pulling him closer.

Varsha watched in disbelief as Vinod turned to her and said, "I am so sorry, please forgive me."

Without another word, Vinod ran off with the girl, both of them climbing into the van. As the van reversed, more chairs were knocked over and plants were damaged. The driver then steered the van towards the gate and sped away, leaving Varsha standing there in shock, abandoned at the altar.

As the chaos unfolded below, the parents of both families came together, their voices rising in a heated argument.

Varsha, still standing on the podium, felt a wave of embarrassment wash over her. Below, event organizers rushed to restore order, placing fallen flower vases back in their positions and repairing damaged ice sculptures.

Varsha watched the commotion from her vantage point, feeling overwhelmed by the turn of events. She couldn't help but feel a deep sense of humiliation as she observed the scene unfolding below.

All of a sudden, another van appeared at the scene. This time, it was yellow and boldly advertised 'The Kidnappers Van' on its exterior. As the van reversed through the gate, Vedant struggled to keep it on course, zigzagging and knocking down flower vases, ice sculptures, and chairs in its path. Event organizers, who had been busy repairing the decorations, quickly scattered from the area.

The yellow van eventually came to a stop in front of the podium, but this time, its back was facing the platform. With the doors flung open, Samrat leaped out and climbed onto the podium. Falling to his knees, he declared to Varsha, "I've made this daring entry, and I'm here to kidnap you. But I can't do it unless you say yes. I love you, and I want to marry you. Please, come with me."

Varsha's parents were in utter shock, her father exclaiming, "What the hell is going on?"

Varsha gazed at Samrat and responded, "You're late."

Samrat was taken aback by her words, scrambling to his feet as he questioned, "What? Have you already gotten married?"

Varsha clarified, "No... but Vinod was kidnapped by his girlfriend, and I was left at the altar."

Samrat found himself in a state of confusion. He glanced back at the van where Nikhil and Priya stood, holding the back doors of the van, they made a gesture to get her in. Turning back to Varsha, he uttered, "Better late than never." Taking her hand, they dashed down the podium and entered the back of the van, with Nikhil and Priya following suit and shutting the doors behind them.

Vedant wasted no time, hitting the accelerator as the van sped past the astonished guests, family, and friends. everyone sees the bold writing on the van 'The Kidnappers Van,' catching the attention of all as it makes its exit through the gates of Varsha's wedding venue.

SIX

A WEDDING INVITATION.

Malavika was at home, fidgeting with impatience. She glanced at her watch, then out the window. The wait for Vedant seemed endless. Restless, she finally decided to take action.

She stormed out, marching straight to the car. Grabbing the red cover, she pulled it off in one swift motion. The satin slid away, revealing the gleaming silver birch color of the car underneath. Malavika stood there, struck by its beauty.

"This Aston Martin lookalike is too good to be called fake," she thought to herself.

She circled the car, admiring its spoke wheels and black leather interior. Each step filled her with disbelief at how stunning it looked.

As she walked around, she noticed something unusual. The window glass was down, and the car was unlocked. Malavika hesitated for a moment, then curiosity got the better of her.

She opened the door and settled into the driver's seat. Her hands gripped the steering wheel, feeling its smoothness. Her eyes wandered to the ignition key, beckoning her.

With a quick decision, she turned the key and the engine roared to life. Malavika felt a rush of excitement, a chill running down her spine.

Unable to resist any longer, she decided to take the car for a spin.

"Wow," she muttered to herself, "this is incredible."

And with that, she drove off into the empty streets of her area and her heart was racing with every turn of the wheel.

Meanwhile, Vedant brought the van back to the restaurant. They all stepped out, and Samrat took Varsha's hand, leading her towards the restaurant.

"Varsha, remember I told you I don't prefer arranged marriage and that I want to fall in love?" Samrat's voice was filled with sincerity.

Varsha looked at Samrat, a smile spreading across her face. "Yes," she replied softly.

Samrat returned her smile, his eyes shining with affection. "Varsha, I love you. I love everything about you, your art, your work, everything."

Varsha's heart skipped a beat, overwhelmed with emotion. "Samrat..." she began, but he continued.

"I want you to work side by side with me, your workshop next to my restaurant here. So, will you be my partner for life?" Samrat's words were filled with hope and love.

Varsha's eyes glistened with tears of joy as she threw her arms around him in a warm embrace. "Yes, Samrat. Yes, I will," she whispered, her voice filled with love and happiness.

Meanwhile, Vedant watched the scene unfold with a heart full of joy. He glanced at Nikhil and Priya, who were now holding hands, their eyes speaking volumes.

"Guys, you both have finally made it," Vedant remarked, his voice filled with pride and happiness.

Samrat approached Vedant, gratitude evident in his eyes. "You were in the midst of proposing to Malavika, and you left everything to help me. I can't thank you enough. We would love to come with you. I'll explain everything to Malavika. I'm sure she'll understand why you ran off."

But Vedant shook his head, determination in his eyes. "No, I want to do this alone. I must leave before it gets too late."

Samrat handed him the keys to the van, a gesture of appreciation. "Thank you for the van. It's very special to me. It has not only helped me build my restaurant but also helped me get Varsha."

Vedant smiled warmly. "Keep the van. Consider it your wedding gift. I must leave now."

With a sense of purpose, Vedant began to run, his heart filled with hope for a positive result. "Wish me luck!" he shouted, his voice echoing in the air as he disappeared into the distance.

Vedant rushed to Malavika's house, his heart pounding with anticipation. As he arrived, he noticed the absence of the car and the car cover lying on the floor. With a furrowed brow, he entered the house, picking up the car cover. But before he could comprehend the situation, Malavika arrived, driving the car herself.

His eyes widened in shock as he watched her park the car and step out. Malavika slammed the car door shut and turned to face Vedant.

"Frankly, I thought I would bring it back before you return," she said, her tone nonchalant.

Vedant sighed, feeling guilty. "I'm sorry I had to leave like this. We had to rush to Varsha's wedding."

Malavika didn't want him to know that she had overheard him on the phone early morning, so she feigned ignorance, her expression shifting to one of surprise. "You left all this to go to a wedding?"

Vedant nodded, a small smile playing on his lips. "Yes, we went there to kidnap Varsha."

Her eyes widened, jaws dropping in disbelief. Vedant hurried to explain, "But everything is okay now. She is with Samrat."

Malavika's expression softened as she processed the information. Vedant took a deep breath, gathering his courage.

"Malavika, I know you're hurt, and I know you are dealing with your brother's death," he began earnestly. "But there is so much love in you. Your heart is kind and beautiful, just like you are. I am madly in love with you, and I made this car out of love for you."

He knelt before her, his eyes pleading. "I don't have a ring, but I have this car. I built it with my own hands. Please accept it. Malavika, I love you, and I want to marry you. So, will you marry me?"

Malavika stood there, stunned by Vedant's heartfelt confession.

"I thought I'd take this car for a ride then bring it back and cover it up again and you will never know I took it out for a ride, but now that you know, I would like to tell you that I am keeping the car," Malavika confessed.

Vedant was taken aback, his astonishment evident as he stood up. "So does that mean..." he trailed off, his mind racing with possibilities.

But Malavika interrupted him, her voice soft but resolute. "Yes... I guess it's time for me to move on."

Vedant couldn't contain his joy at her decision. "Can I hug you?" he asked eagerly.

Malavika hesitated for a moment before responding, "No... let it sink in first."

Undeterred, Vedant flashed a bright smile and rushed forward, enveloping her in a tight embrace. After a brief moment, he released her, holding her hands gently. "Thank you for accepting me," he expressed sincerely.

Initially shocked by his sudden affection, Malavika soon found herself smiling back at him.

Vedant smiled back, his stomach growling in hunger. "I haven't eaten anything since morning," he admitted sheepishly.

Malavika's smile widened, and she took Vedant by the hand, leading him inside. "Come, I'll make you some breakfast. By the way, I heard you talk on the phone this morning, tell me everything from the start."

"About the wedding? You won't believe what happened," Vedant replied, his excitement evident in his voice.

Vedant entered the house with Malavika, narrating the story of the wedding. As he spoke, his words painted a vivid picture of the events that unfolded, captivating Malavika's attention.

And so, finally, even Vedant managed to win Malavika's heart as well.

A week later, everyone gathered at Malavika's house. Vedant piped up, "We have another long weekend. How about a trip to Goa, but this time with our girlfriends?"

Samrat readily agreed, "Yes, why not?"

Varsha chuckled, "Your restaurant is brand new, and now you don't work for anyone, so there is no weekend for you."

Samrat reassured her, "Relax, I can take care of it."

Nikhil chimed in, "It is a good idea."

However, Priya seemed hesitant. "Sorry guys, I won't make it. Mom will never allow me to go."

Nikhil was determined, "We'll think of something, but you have to come."

Just then, Malavika emerged from the kitchen and joined the conversation. Nikhil turned to her, suggesting, "Malavika will help. She'll talk to your mother."

Malavika tapped Priya's back reassuringly and said, "I'll help, but we are not going to Goa this time."

Vedant, puzzled, asked, "But we always go to Goa. It's like a ritual now."

Malavika's response was unexpected. "Consider this your first experience. Whenever a woman enters your life, your life will never be the same. There will always be some changes that will take place."

Vedant, Samrat, and Nikhil were left dumbstruck, staring at Malavika in astonishment.

Varsha teased, "Don't scare them with your reality check."

Malavika chuckled, "Relax, guys, I am just kidding. My best friend Rukmini is getting married this weekend, and she has invited us to her wedding. So, instead of this Goa trip, how about a road trip to Kerala?"

Excitement filled the air as Vedant exclaimed, "Rukmini told me she'll settle down soon. Besides, a trip is a trip. Why not? Let's go to Kerala, guys!"

Everyone eagerly agreed to this new plan, their hearts brimming with anticipation for the upcoming adventure.

Vedant suggested, "I can arrange a bigger SUV. We'll have fun."

Nikhil chimed in, "I have something in mind."

Curious, Malavika asked, "What is it?"

Nikhil explained his idea, "I have traveled a lot on my scooter and done plenty of camping alone. So, I have experience traveling long distances on my scooter. I feel, why don't Priya and I take the scooter? Vedant and Malavika can take their new car, and obviously, Samrat the kidnapper can take Varsha along in his van. We can all drive together. What do you think?"

Samrat expressed concern, "But your scooter is a vintage."

Nikhil reassured him, "Yes, but it has a new engine, so no worries."

Varsha supported the idea, "I think it's a good idea. We all get to drive our special ride."

Priya added, "We'll have to plan the trip if we are going by road."

Malavika took charge, "I have planned everything. We will leave at five, early morning and by eight in the evening, we'll halt at some hotel for the night. Then, we'll leave early the next day, and by night, we'll reach Kerala and the day after that, we can attend Rukmini's wedding."

Later that day, at Priya's house, it took almost two hours for Malavika and Varsha to convince Priya's mother to let Priya come to the wedding. Eventually, she agreed.

The very next early morning, the gang left Mumbai and headed towards Kerala by road. Malavika drove her new car with Vedant beside her, Samrat drove his van along with Varsha, and Priya rode on Nikhil's scooter with Nikhil seated behind her.

They had fun on the road, halting many times for breaks and enjoying the beautiful scenery. By nightfall, they halted at a hotel where the girls stayed in one room and the boys in another. The next morning, they hit the road again, and they finally reached Kerala at night.

The gang stayed at Malavika's place after reaching Kerala. It was Vedant's first time meeting Malavika's parents, but the meeting was brief due to the late hour, and they had to rise early the next day for the wedding.

The following day dawned, marking the wedding day. Everyone dressed up for the occasion. The boys donned kurtas and pajamas, while Varsha and Malavika elegantly draped traditional sarees. Priya opted for a crop top paired with a similarly styled ethnic skirt.

At the wedding venue, they encountered Rukmini, the bride, who was delighted to see Vedant and Malavika together. However, due to the wedding proceedings, they couldn't spend much time with her. The ceremony took place near a temple, adorned with a plethora of flowers.

Following the wedding rituals, a sumptuous meal was served on banana leaves. Various vegetarian dishes graced the banana leaf, emitting tantalizing aromas. After the satisfying lunch, musical performances entertained the guests, bringing joy and merriment to the occasion. The festivities culminated by seven in the evening, leaving everyone with fond memories of the celebration.

Everyone cherished the experience of this traditional wedding. Malavika then led the gang back to her house, where they spent the rest of the evening in each other's company.

The next morning, while having breakfast together, Priya exclaimed, "I want to see the elephants."

Nikhil quickly agreed, "Me too."

Malavika offered, "I'll give you an address. There is this place called Elephants Junction where elephants are taken care of. You can experience a close encounter with the elephants there."

Samrat chimed in, "I want to experience the houseboats."

Vedant teased, "I know what you want to experience."

Varsha shot Samrat a stare, prompting him to quickly clarify, "Just a day tour in the houseboat, Yaar."

Malavika intervened, "Don't pay attention to him. My friend owns a houseboat here. It won't be free, but you'll definitely get a discount. I'll call him and tell him that you're coming. You can go there after breakfast."

Vedant looked at Malavika and asked, "What about us?"

Samrat retorted, "You're not getting anything until you properly grow up."

Annoyed, Vedant glanced at Samrat.

Malavika then revealed their plan, "We are going for a swim. I have a secret hideout and no one will be around because it's private property. Best waterfall and clear water. I hope you know how to swim."

Vedant confirmed, "Yes, I can swim."

Priya added mischievously, "Yes, but can you swim faster? I've heard the crocodiles here are very quick."

Slightly scared, Vedant questioned, "Crocodiles?"

Malavika reassured him, "There are no crocodiles, but can you jump from a four-story high cliff?"

Vedant, now concerned, asked, "Jump from a cliff?"

Nikhil joked, "That's it. If you survive the jump, you'll be eaten alive by alligators below."

Vedant, now thoroughly alarmed, asked, "Alligators?"

Malavika teased, "Don't forget your swimming trunks."

Vedant hesitated, "I don't think it's safe. Are you sure you want to go for a swim?"

Malavika, undeterred, asserted, "I have been going there since I was a child and as you can see, I am still alive."

Priya, curious, asked Malavika, "Are you going to wear a bikini?"

Malavika replied cheekily, "Yes, and if you're wondering if it's one piece or two, then I might try the new two-piece bikini I just bought," giving Vedant a playful glance.

Vedant abruptly got up from the table and said, "I'll go get ready," rushing back to his room. Everyone burst into laughter at the table.

After breakfast, Priya and Nikhil hopped onto their scooter and zoomed off to the place Malavika had mentioned. As they arrived, they were greeted by a towering gate, adorned with a bell. Priya, with a playful grin, reached out and pulled the string, sending a melodious chime through the air.

"Wow, this place looks amazing!" Priya exclaimed as they entered the premises. Two elephants peacefully grazed nearby, adding a serene charm to the surroundings.

"I know! Look at all this greenery," Nikhil remarked, taking in the lush park.

Soon, the caretakers of the park joined them, and after making payments at the counter, they embarked on a guided tour. Priya, being a vlogger with permission, whipped out her GoPro camera to capture every moment. Nikhil was now equipped with the GoPro Priya had handed him and he eagerly recorded her every move.

"This place is incredible!" Priya narrated to her audience, her excitement palpable.

The caretakers introduced them to some of the resident elephants, a total of five majestic creatures. They explained the elephants' diet and even brought out some fruits and vegetables for feeding.

Priya struggled to reach the elephant's mouth, but Nikhil, with his tall frame, managed to feed the gentle giant.

Next, they were led to the bathing area, where one of the caretakers was gently scrubbing an elephant. The elephant lay peacefully, enjoying the attention.

"Nikhil, why don't you give it a try?" Priya suggested, nudging him playfully.

Nikhil hesitated for a moment but soon found himself enjoying the experience of scrubbing the elephant's tough hide.

Later, the caretaker instructed the elephant to sit down, inviting Priya to climb aboard. With a mix of excitement and anxiety, Priya settled onto the elephant's back. The majestic creature then began its bath, filling its trunk with water and playfully splashing it over its back, drenching Priya in the process.

Nikhil, capturing the moment with his GoPro, couldn't help but chuckle at the sight. "You're getting quite the shower there, Priya!"

"It's so much fun!" Priya laughed, her clothes now thoroughly soaked.

Nikhil, seeing Priya's having all the fun, decided to join her. With a grin, he approached the elephant, ready for his experience of the refreshing shower.

As the elephant sprayed water over Nikhil, the two of them shared a moment of pure joy, both soaked from head to toe.

"That was incredible!" Priya exclaimed, her hair dripping with water.

Nikhil nodded, grinning from ear to ear. "this is definitely a once-in-a-lifetime experience."

The caretaker, watching with amusement, reassured them, "Don't worry about getting wet. I know how to dry off in the sun."

So, the caretaker, with a warm smile, decided to treat them to an elephant ride. As they climbed onto the elephant's back, a new adventure awaited them. Riding on the elephant was a whole new experience, as they meandered through the plantation, basking in the warmth of the sun.

"It feels so peaceful up here," Priya remarked, her hair gently swaying in the breeze.

Nikhil nodded in agreement, "Yeah, it's like we're part of nature."

Overall, Nikhil and Priya found the experience to be incredibly fulfilling. They were delighted to see how well the elephants were cared for in this sanctuary.

"We should definitely come back here sometime," Nikhil suggested, his face beaming with satisfaction.

Priya nodded enthusiastically, "Absolutely! It's so heartwarming to see these gentle giants living happily."

With memories captured on Priya's GoPro, they bid farewell to the caretakers and prepared for their next adventure.

Before they departed, the caretaker offered them a suggestion, "You two should check out the spice garden retreat. It's a place young couples like you will enjoy."

Excited by the prospect of another adventure, Nikhil and Priya hopped onto their Lambretta and set off towards the spice garden.

As they arrived, they were greeted by a picturesque entryway, with a charming wooden bridge leading them to the main lobby.

Inside, everything was adorned with natural elements, giving it a cozy yet elegant feel. A friendly lady was there to welcome Nikhil and Priya, eager to show them around the property.

She took them around the farm, showcasing the diverse range of plantations they nurtured.

"If you stay for the night," she enthused, "you'll truly get to soak in the essence of this place. And the food! Oh, it's a treat prepared by our local chefs. You won't find such delicious home-cooked meals anywhere else. We prepare both vegetarian and non-vegetarian dishes, all sourced straight from our farm. "We grow everything here," she explained proudly, "and our kitchen uses only the freshest vegetables from our gardens. We even have our own animal farm!"

You'll be treated to lunch and dinner, with evening snacks and drinks to accompany. And before you check out in the morning, we'll serve you a hearty breakfast."

Nikhil and Priya exchanged a look, the prospect of indulging in such wholesome meals and experiencing the tranquility of the place making their decision to stay for the night even more enticing.

She insisted on giving them a tour of the small cottages for guests. Each one was a rustic haven, adorned with vintage charm that immediately appealed to Priya.

"Why don't we spend some time here?" she suggested to Nikhil.

The lady chimed in, "You can book a cottage and I'll show you around. After some rest, you can enjoy lunch together. In the evening, we have a gardening activity for all our guests. Later, you can unwind in our game area or watch a movie in the common room, and you can check out in the morning after breakfast."

"I think we should go for it," Priya said, excitement twinkling in her eyes.

Nikhil agreed, "Okay, if you say so. Let's book a cottage. But make sure to call Malavika and let her know we won't be coming for the night. And please, don't spill the beans about the cottage. Just tell her it's some open camp thing or whatever," he added, a smirk playing on his lips.

Priya couldn't help but giggle at Nikhil's antics.

Nikhil and Priya had a blast all day long. The food was delicious, the atmosphere serene, bringing them close to nature's heart. As night fell, they found themselves on the porch of their cozy cottage, swaying gently on a large wooden swing.

Priya gazed out, murmuring, "Wow, this is so romantic."

Nikhil, feeling the magic of the moment, asked softly, "When do you think we'll get married?"

Priya pondered for a moment before responding, "Soon I'll be 20, so... maybe when I turn 21 or after college, I suppose."

Nikhil regarded Priya with affection and remarked, "This feels almost like a honeymoon for us."

Priya, with a playful smile, teased, "Almost?"

Nikhil's expression shifted to surprise as he processed her words.

Priya laughed, pulling him up from the swing, "Come on, let's go inside. By morning, that 'almost' will disappear."

Nikhil, intrigued, asked, "What do you mean by that?"

With a giggle, Priya revealed, "I knew you wouldn't come prepared, so don't worry, I brought 'raincoat' along."

"Raincoat?" Nikhil echoed, bewildered.

Priya simply giggled and tugged him into their cottage room, leaving the tranquil night behind them.

Malavika had promised Vedant an adventure, a journey to a secret hideout. She drove him to a place owned by her uncle, who possessed vast acres of land. Their first stop was her uncle's grand residence, though he was away on a business tour, the caretakers were familiar with Malavika and welcomed them warmly. Malavika told the caretakers they were going out for a swim and would be back for lunch in the afternoon.

Together, Malavika and Vedant wandered through the open meadows for quite some time until they reached their destination.

"Listen carefully," Malavika said, her voice tinged with excitement. "Can you hear something?"

Vedant strained his ears and suggested, "A waterfall?"

With a nod of confirmation, Malavika led him further until they stood on the edge of a cliff.

Below them, a small lake glistened, fed by a cascading waterfall from the clear stream running through the fields above.

"I would have never guessed we were standing on top of a cliff. Everything looked so flat around here," Vedant marveled.

Grinning, Malavika revealed, "This is my favorite hidden spot. We're going down there for a swim."

Perplexed, Vedant asked, "But how are we going to get down there?"

Unfazed, Malavika began to undress, stuffing her clothes and shoes into a duffel bag. As she revealed herself in a yellow bikini, Vedant couldn't help but gaze at her, captivated by her beauty.

Malavika turned to Nikhil and instructed, "Take off your clothes and shoes. I hope you're wearing your swim trunks under those pants." Vedant swiftly complied, revealing his swimming trunks beneath his pants. Malavika stuffed his clothes and shoes into the duffel bag before striding to the edge of the cliff.

With a determined toss, she hurled the bag below.

Vedant, startled by her action, rushed to the edge to catch a glimpse. Below, the bag lay on the ground next to the lake, surrounded by lush greenery and towering trees.

The waterfall, though not powerful, cast a gentle rainbow as sunlight danced upon it. The lake's crystal-clear water sparkled invitingly, though its depth seemed daunting.

"How do we get down there?" Vedant queried, his eyes fixed on the serene scene below.

Suddenly, the thumping sound of footsteps reached his ears. Turning, Vedant watched as Malavika swiftly passed him and leaped into the water below, creating a resounding splash.

Dumbstruck, Vedant stared at the water, disbelief washing over him as Malavika emerged from its depths.

"Jump... it's just four stories high," Malavika called up to him.

"Four stories high?" Vedant murmured incredulously.

He hesitated, grappling with fear and uncertainty. He couldn't believe he was expected to take such a leap. But as he weighed his options, he knew that if he backed out, Malavika would undoubtedly tease him endlessly.

Summoning every ounce of courage, Vedant took a deep breath and launched himself into the air. With a resounding splash, he broke through the surface of the lake, sinking down to its depths. It took him a moment to orient himself and rise back to the surface.

"Are you okay?" Malavika called out, concern lacing her voice.

Vedant flashed a thumbs-up, still adjusting to the sensation of the dive. Gradually, he acclimated to the water and began to relish the freedom and joy of swimming in the tranquil lake.

Vedant and Malavika lost track of time as they swam for hours in the tranquil lake, utterly enchanted by the serene surroundings. The only sounds they heard were the whispers of nature itself.

"We should take a break," Malavika suggested.

"Yeah," Vedant agreed, beginning to swim towards the green patch where their bag lay.

But Malavika had other plans. "Wait, not there. Follow me," she directed, swimming towards the waterfall.

Curious, Vedant followed her lead. As Malavika disappeared behind the cascading water, Vedant realized there was a hidden alcove behind the waterfall.

He swam towards it, finding himself in a cave bathed in sunlight filtering through the waterfall. Smooth, rounded rocks filled the space, and Malavika was already resting on one of the rocks, watching as Vedant swam in through the waterfall. Vedant stopped and looked at Malavika sitting on the rock, then swam towards her and climbed onto the slippery surface. The rocks resembled giant pebbles smoothed over by years of water flow. Vedant settled next to Malavika, observing her shivering and her chattering teeth. he asked, "Are you cold?"

"No, I'm warming up slowly," Malavika replied.

Taking in the breathtaking view of the waterfall, Vedant remarked, "You were right; this place is amazing."

"I've planned this for a long time. I wanted to share this place with you," Malavika confessed, her eyes sparkling with anticipation.

Vedant smiled at her and planted a gentle kiss on her cheek. Malavika met his gaze, still slightly breathless, her teeth lightly chattering. "Have you seen those movies where the actors kiss underwater?" she asked.

Vedant nodded. "Yes... Do you want to kiss under the water?"

Malavika smiled, turning her gaze towards the waterfall without a word.

Vedant, sensing the need for a change of topic, asked, "By the way, you showed me how to come down here. I'm curious to know, how do we climb back up there?"

Malavika chuckled mischievously.

"I've had enough surprises for one day. Please don't give me a heart attack by telling me we have to climb our way back up to the top," said Vedant.

Standing up on the rock, Malavika grinned. "Let's see if your heart can take this."

"What are you up to now?" Vedant asked, feeling a mixture of anticipation and nervousness.

"I dare you to take a skinny dip," Malavika declared boldly.

"What?" Vedant exclaimed, taken aback.

Without hesitation, Malavika untied the string of her bikini and let it drop onto the stone, she looked stunning. Vedant's heart raced as he struggled to comprehend the situation unfolding before him.

"What if anybody comes?" he stammered, his voice betraying his apprehension.

"This is private property, and besides, we're in a cave behind a waterfall," Malavika reassured him with a playful smile.

With a splash, Malavika jumped into the water. Surfacing, she called out to Vedant, "Aren't you coming?"

Feeling a mix of excitement and embarrassment, Vedant slowly entered the water.

"Skinny dip? Get rid of your trunks," Malavika teased.

Too shy to remove his trunks in front of her, Vedant slipped them off underwater and tossed them onto the rock.

Malavika pulled him closer and whispered, "I want to know how it feels to kiss underwater."

Speechless, Vedant simply nodded, following Malavika's lead. As they submerged beneath the water's surface, Malavika's hair spread out around her like a mermaid's, adding to her ethereal beauty. Pulling him close, she kissed him passionately, their underwater embrace punctuated by playful air bubbles before giving way to a deeper connection as they savored their intimate moment beneath the surface.

A little while later, they found themselves standing on the lush green grass near the lake, the same spot where Malavika had thrown the bag. Vedant, holding a towel below him, struggled to change out of his wet trunks, while Malavika had already swapped her clothes for a t-shirt and shorts, busy drying her hair with her towel.

Seeing Vedant's difficulty, she teased, "You were naked in front of me a little while ago."

Vedant glanced at her and replied sheepishly, "That was different."

After much effort, Vedant finally managed to put on his shorts and t-shirt.

Looking at Malavika, who was now holding the duffel bag, Vedant asked, "Now tell me, how do we get up there?"

Malavika took Vedant's arm and led him straight into the dense trees that loomed in the background. After a brief two-minute walk among the trees, they emerged into an open clearing, where they could see her uncle's massive house in the distance. Vedant was taken aback.

"If this was so close, how did we end up on the top of that cliff?"

"We took the long way around and hiked the other way to reach the top," Malavika explained with a grin.

Vedant stopped walking, his jaw dropping in disbelief. Malavika teased, "Come on, admit it. You enjoyed that jump, didn't you?"

Vedant tried to suppress a smile, but it broke through. "It's 4 o'clock. Do you think they'll save us some lunch?"

Grabbing Vedant's arm again, Malavika assured him, "Don't worry, we have a feast waiting for us."

After a hearty meal at her uncle's house, they relaxed for a while before heading back to Malavika's place.

Samrat and Varsha were aboard a houseboat, accompanied by two other newlywed couples. They had booked the full-day slot, a tad pricey but thanks to Malavika's referral, they snagged a hefty discount. The houseboat was a marvel, boasting two spacious decks—one at the bow and another at the stern. The captain manned the wheel at the front, navigating the vessel through the winding backwaters.

Behind the captain, there was a cozy lounge adorned with a huge TV and comfy love seats. Adjacent to it was a six-seater dining area. In the middle of the boat, there were three separate rooms.

The middle room was allocated to Samrat and Varsha, furnished with all the amenities, it rivaled a three-star hotel room, complete with ensuite facilities. Moving forward, they found the kitchen where the crew members were already busy preparing a meal.

"Wow, Varsha, isn't this incredible?" Samrat exclaimed, his eyes sparkling with excitement.

Varsha nodded, a wide grin spreading across her face. "Yeah, it's beyond what I imagined."

As music filled the air, the crew circulated with snacks and refreshing coconut water.

For Samrat and Varsha, it was a first-time experience, and they relished every moment. They spent hours on the deck, entranced by the serene backwaters and the lush greenery flanking the river.

As they settled into their seats, Samrat couldn't help but feel grateful for Malavika's recommendation. It was turning out to be an unforgettable day on the backwaters.

Soon, the other couples became friends, and it felt as though they were all on this trip together. The boat halted at several places for sightseeing, and during lunch, an array of seafood dishes was served. The table boasted a good spread: fried pomfret, roasted crab, fried tiger prawns, chicken curry, parathas, and rice.

After indulging in the delicious meal, they hung out on the front deck of the boat. By 6 in the evening, the boat came to a halt. Samrat, Varsha, and their newly made friends enjoyed the beautiful sunset on the deck of the boat. As darkness descended, the lights on the boat illuminated brightly, and music filled the air as snacks and drinks were served.

The crew even brought out a local beverage called toddy, a refreshing, mildly alcoholic drink made by fermenting the sap of the coconut palm. Everyone savored the drink, and soon, one of the couples started dancing. Varsha and Samrat couldn't resist joining in, swaying to the music.

The other couple seemed a bit shy but cheered enthusiastically for the dancers. They continued dancing until late, with even the crew cheering them on. As the night wore on, dinner was served, bringing an end to a magical day on the backwaters.

Later that night, after dinner, Varsha called Malavika to thank her and inform her they'd be arriving the next day.

The boat crew promised an early start to catch the beautiful sunrise. Varsha and Samrat found themselves sharing a room for the first time, which was a bit awkward for them both. As they settled in, the passing boats created ripples, rocking their boat like a cradle.

Varsha, clad in her pajamas, nervously sat next to Samrat on the bed. Suddenly, they heard squeaking from the next room. Samrat pointed to the wall, and they both rushed to listen closely. The unmistakable sounds of squeaking and moaning reached their ears. Varsha bit her fist to stifle her laughter, while Samrat struggled to contain his amusement, covering his mouth.

Unable to hold back, Varsha burst into giggles, covering her mouth as well. "Let's check the other wall," she suggested. They hurried across the room and pressed their ears against the opposite wall. Though the sounds were fainter, they could still make out some activity.

"Wow, these couples are pros, keeping it quiet," Samrat remarked, impressed. Varsha pulled Samrat back to the bed, and as they sat together, Samrat's gaze wandered toward the other wall. Even from their bed, they could still hear the faint squeaking sounds echoing through the room.

Now that they were aware of the other two couples engaging in intimate activities in their rooms, Varsha turned to Samrat and asked, "Are you expecting something to happen?"

Samrat glanced at her and replied, "Well, I'm not going to make a move unless you want something to happen."

"Can we wait till marriage?" Varsha inquired.

With a smile, Samrat responded, "Sure, we can wait. But promise me you'll do some of those things you drew in your graphic novel."

Varsha chuckled, "Oh, so you want a role-play? I'll do something even better, I'll get those costumes as well."

Samrat's eyebrows shot up, his jaw dropping slightly as he tried to maintain a smile. Varsha couldn't help but tease, "You've been reading those erotic manga, haven't you?"

Chuckling, Samrat confessed, "Only the one you gave me."

Later on, as they drifted off to sleep, Varsha snuggled up to Samrat in bed. Slowly, Samrat turned to look at Varsha, noticing how she had nestled herself. Her leg rested atop his, her hands tightly wrapped around his waist, and her face buried into his neck. Varsha seemed completely unaware of how she had fallen asleep, but Samrat couldn't help but feel a sense of warmth and contentment.

This was all new for Samrat; he had never slept like this before. Despite feeling a bit uncomfortable, he found himself overwhelmed with happiness. Unable to move due to Varsha's tight grip, Samrat lay there, cherishing the moment, realizing he had never experienced anything quite like it before.

Malavika and Vedant arrived home, parking her car in the corner of the front yard. As Malavika covered her car with the same cover Vedant had given her, Vedant couldn't help but smile, watching her do it on her own. With the car taken care of, Vedant glanced back at the house, noticing the unusual quietness. "Looks like the gang hasn't returned yet," he remarked.

Malavika's smile widened as she replied, "They'll be back in the morning."

Raising his eyebrows, Vedant questioned, "Are you saying they're staying for the night?"

Malavika's smile grew even brighter. "You sound jealous; I guess they came prepared."

Vedant pondered for a moment before asking, "You mean they planned all this?"

Malavika shrugged playfully. "Maybe, or maybe it was a spur-of-the-moment thing."

Malavika sat on the front porch stairs of her house, and Vedant joined her. They sat together in the darkness, gazing up at the moon above. "Are you regretting not doing it?" Malavika asked.

Vedant turned to look at Malavika, pondering her question before responding, "Are you?"

Malavika chuckled softly. "No, I never thought about doing it. I just had a great time. By the way, how did I look?"

Vedant's gaze softened as he replied, "Above the water, you were like a tall marble statue of a Greek goddess."

Malavika raised her eyebrows, intrigued. "And under the water?"

Vedant's voice was filled with admiration as he answered, "You were like a mermaid, the most beautiful thing I ever saw."

Blushing, Malavika smiled, feeling touched by Vedant's words. Vedant continued, his tone earnest, "No one on this planet is lucky enough to experience this. Today's day has left an imprint on my heart, and I'll remember this day forever."

Feeling a surge of emotion, Malavika grabbed Vedant's arm and leaned over him. But their intimate moment was interrupted as Malavika's mom opened the door, causing them to quickly move away, startled by the intrusion.

Malavika's mom called them inside, urging them to come in for dinner. She walked back into the house, announcing that dinner was almost ready and instructing them to get inside and freshen up.

"Though my real parents are no more, they have taken good care of me, and I guess now is the right time for you to make a good impression," Malavika remarked to Vedant.

Later, at the dinner table, Vedant sat with Malavika's family, engaging in lively conversation and bonding well with them. It was evident that they liked him, and Malavika couldn't help but feel happy seeing how quickly Vedant had become a part of her family. She felt grateful that her parents approved of him.

Malavika picked up the empty dishes from the table and carried them into the kitchen. She placed them in the kitchen sink, glancing up at the window above. Through it, she gazed out towards the sky. As the night drew to a close and the stars twinkled in the sky, Malavika couldn't help but reflect on the beautiful moments shared with Vedant and the warmth of her family's approval. With a heart full of gratitude and happiness, she knew that this was just the beginning of their journey together, filled with love, laughter, and cherished memories yet to be made.

THE END.

What happened after this trip?

There were no more Goa trips for the gang.

Samrat and Varsha got busy with their work, and six months later, they got married, they had to do a court marriage since her father refused to spend any money on a wedding.

The gang had to make a second trip to Kerala after a year, this time it was Vedant and Malavika's wedding.

And what about Nikhil and Priya?

It had been a while since their last trip to Goa, So Nikhil came up with a plan to convince Priya for a wedding in Goa. Priya asked him, 'What will I get if I agree?'

Nikhil handed her the keys to his Lambretta and said, 'My dad gifted this to my mom, and now I am giving this to you, a gift of love.' Priya was very emotional, and tears welled up in her eyes. Priya reminisced, 'Remember how we first met, this scooter brought us close together.'

Soon, Priya's mother agreed, and for Nikhil, it was a surprise that Priya's mom agreed to their relationship. When Priya turned 22, they planned their marriage, and guess where? They planned to get married in Goa. Later, they found out that Priya's mom was in a relationship with a guy younger than her, and since she didn't want any trouble, she agreed to their wedding.

The long-time ritual that was broken by the girls finally got back on track. Everyone traveled together to Goa for Nikhil's and Priya's wedding, this time in a mini-bus. And not to forget the ritual, the inaugural track for their song was none other than the title song from the movie 'Dil Chahta Hai.'

No end to this love trip.

www.ingramcontent.com/pod-product-compliance
Lightning Source LLC
LaVergne TN
LVHW091059150826
845673LV00002B/648

* 9 7 9 8 8 9 3 6 3 0 0 6 0 *